Trolley Dodgers

Trolley Dodgers

Jeff Stanger

THE WRITERS' COLLECTIVE
Independent Books for Independent Readers

Cover Designer: Robert Aulicino
Interior Design: Mary Jo Zazueta

ISBN-13: 978-1-59411-083-2
ISBN-10: 1-59411-083-2

Library of Congress Control Number: 2004095938

Printed in the United States of America

10 9 8 7 6 5 4 3 2 1

Published by The Writers' Collective ▲ Cranston, Rhode Island

TROLLEY DODGERS HALL OF FAME

ALL STAR EDITING TEAM

Thanks to my editing team: Bonnie Hearn Hill (content), C.E. Gatchalian, Terry Sowka and Jeanette Baker (copy), and Lorrie Algate (color and shape).

SCOUTING AND FRONT OFFICE SUPPORT

Many people contributed with research, advice, and encouragement. I greatly appreciate the contributions made by: Darryl Neher, Matt Algate, Brian Groce, Linda Toupin, Mary Kay, Inc., Mark Shumacher, the Indianapolis Indians, BoDeans, Milt Thompson, Mike Lennox and Angie Kohlmeier.

SEASON TICKET HOLDERS

Special thanks to my family and friends who kept this project alive.

LEAGUE MVP

Finally, thanks to Lorrie Algate for being an editor, coach, cheerleader, and friend.

PROLOGUE

I REMEMBER THE DAY I SAW THE SHOOTING STARS. Darryl and I were twelve. We were playing catch at Roxy's house. I remember throwing the ball over Darryl's head and watching it roll into the bushes. The sun was going down behind the trees that lined the back of Roxy's lot. We walked towards the golden sky to look for the ball. After a few minutes of looking, we found the baseball and turned our backs to the sunset to continue playing catch. That's when we saw them.

"Make a wish," Darryl said. Both of us closed our eyes, and made twelve-year-old wishes.

"What did you wish for?" I asked.

"To be a baseball player."

"Me too."

"Look, there's another one!" Darryl shouted. "Make another wish."

I closed my eyes and wished as hard as I could.

"Now what did you wish for?"

"I wished we had a baseball team in Bloomington," I said.

Darryl looked puzzled at first, as if the idea had never crossed his mind. Then his face lit up. "Wow. I wish I would have thought of that. Well, I'm sure it will come true. It has to."

Darryl was just as sure it would happen as he was that baseball bats were made of wood. Darryl was sure. I said, "I don't know."

Trolley Dodgers

ONE

I Was Kidding

(Money Raised: $0)

"When I was a small boy in Kansas, a friend of mine and I went fishing . . . I told him I wanted to be a real Major League Baseball Player, a genuine professional like Honus Wagner. My friend said that he'd like to be President of the United States. Neither of us got our wish."

~ *Dwight D. Eisenhower*

I SPIT COKE ALL OVER THE MICROPHONE. As it shot through my nose, I slammed my cup down, gasped for breath and feebly attempted to compose myself. Jesse held up his left arm, twisting it frantically towards Darryl, the signal to take a commercial break. To me, he made a neck-slashing gesture using his right hand. I quickly tried to wipe the fizzling brown liquid off the wooden console. All the while, I was still snorting, choking, and coughing.

"Hold that thought, caller, and we'll answer your question after the commercial break. Stay tuned for more of today's controversial topic: Bringing Major League Baseball to Bloomington, Indiana. Our in-studio guest is *Bloomington Daily News* reporter Andy Bennett. Kristy will update the news and weather after the break."

Darryl took off his headset and started laughing. "What's the matter? You know you've opened a can of worms now. These people are ready to do it."

Jesse glared at both of us. Jesse may have been only an intern, but this was definitely *his* sound booth.

"Well, it doesn't help that you're encouraging these wackos," I said. "And why do you keep calling it a 'controversial effort' to bring the Dodgers to Bloomington? There's no effort underway, you tool. I just wrote an article. *I was kidding.*"

"You weren't kidding," Darryl shot back. "You've wanted this all your life. You're just too much of a coward to admit it."

Was Darryl right? The previous caller uttered the one sentence that I never expected to hear. I thought some people would call in and say the article made them laugh. I thought others would say that I wasted seventeen inches of newsprint on a pipe dream. I wasn't prepared for someone to actually call in and say, "I want to invest. Where do I send the money?" That was the question that launched the carbonated shower onto the console.

Why was this caller ready to shell out his life savings? Well, just a week earlier, I was approaching my weekly deadline, and as always, I had no idea how I was going to fill my quota of newsprint for the *Bloomington Daily News*. When I was stumped, I would track down my good buddy Michael Turner. Michael was a chat machine who knew everything about sports. I need only ask one sports question, and three hours, six beers, and four debates later—usually Michael debating himself—I would have a story idea.

On this particular occasion, Michael was ranting and raving because the Los Angeles Dodgers were up for sale. Michael, being an East Coast transplant, was constantly lamenting the Dodgers' move from Brooklyn to Los Angeles in the fifties. He was already talking (to himself) about the Dodgers when I sat down at the bar. Like most Dodger fans, he couldn't bear the thought of his beloved team falling into the hands of some giant corporation. I took a pitcher off the bar, filled his glass with topic juice, and motioned for the waitress, Jenny, to bring me a glass.

Michael was an MIT graduate who had devised a computer ratings system for sports teams. His system was so successful that all the major sports networks paid him royalties. Despite his inherent genius and financial success, he always had a couple of days' worth of facial hair and a raggedy set of clothes. His salt and pepper hair hadn't been combed since the early nineties. On the bar was a faded bag that he carried everywhere he went. I remember having to carry a bag like that when I was in middle school.

He looked me in the eye and whispered, "I think we could do it. I know we could do it. Let me figure this out."

He squinted, tilted his head and started mumbling to himself. He mumbled between sips of beer for about ten minutes. I didn't disturb him. When Michael went off on one of these tangents, it was best to let him be. Most of his words were impossible to make out. Sometimes I could understand a phrase or two. "Twenty thousand dollars . . . all the adults . . . the commissioner would have to cave . . . sell shares . . ."

Then he spoke directly to me. As I look back now, I realize that a light should have been shining down on the two of us at the time. It was Moses coming down from the mountain, or Martin Luther King delivering the "I have a dream" speech, or Gilligan figuring out how to get off the island. The next sentence to come out of his mouth would change an entire town. "If everybody in this county age eighteen or older would borrow $20,000, we could buy the Dodgers."

"Right." I paused, waiting for the punch line. "The Dodgers? The L.A. Dodgers?"

"Absolutely!"

"Jenny, how many pitchers has he had?"

"That's the first one," she called down from the end of the bar.

"Is this topic juice or liquid peyote? Michael's talking gibberish!"

"I am not. We could do it. Jenny, how would you like to own a baseball team?"

"Would the players tip better than you two deadbeats?"

"Sure," we said in unison.

"I'm in," she replied.

"See how easy that was?" Michael said.

"You didn't mention the money," I added.

"What money?" Her enthusiasm halted abruptly.

"You'd need to come up with a rather large investment," Michael said. "But the payoff could be enormous."

"I'll settle for a tip. No more topic juice." She grabbed the pitcher and walked away laughing.

"OK, explain this whole thing to me. How are we going to do this?" I asked.

"We form a publicly owned company, sell shares, you know, a public offering, and use the money to buy the team. Like the Packers are owned by the people of Green Bay. The cost of the team is $250 million. We get everyone in the county to borrow from their local bank and we're set."

"We don't have a stadium," I pointed out.

"We'll build one. We'll leave the team in L.A. while we build a stadium. Hey, you're the one who's always talking about bringing baseball to Bloomington. You should be behind this all the way."

"That was minor league baseball."

"This is the *Dodgers*!"

"OK, you've got me there."

"Jenny, it wouldn't have to be that much," Michael yelled.

Jenny brought back the pitcher and we fortified our juice reserves. "It wouldn't?" she asked.

"No, it wouldn't," I answered. I didn't have that kind of money either. "We could have shares for small time investors, too."

"I like the sound of that," she said.

"Me, too," I replied.

"It's almost happy hour, which means the tipping customers are on their way," she said. "You've got a deadline coming.

You're not seriously going to write about buying a baseball team are you?"

Was Jenny daring or warning me? I took it as a dare. Deep in my heart I wanted a baseball team in Bloomington. However, I always envisioned a minor league team with a small stadium. Michael was talking about the Dodgers—the *L.A. Dodgers*! Were we crazy?

We tossed some cash on the bar and headed outside. Michael said his usual goodbye, which is no goodbye at all. He just wandered off muttering to himself. He left me standing outside on Kirkwood Avenue with a head full of questions.

The next day, I wrote my column. I called the mayor and got a quote from him. I included diagrams of possible stadium locations. I even included a picture of Ebbets Field—where the Dodgers played in Brooklyn—with the mayor's name superimposed on the front of the stadium. I think he really liked the ring of "Gomez Park."

The story was completely tongue-in-cheek, and devoid of facts and research. I hoped it would get a few laughs and maybe get people to one day think about minor league baseball in Bloomington. Instead, a large and quite scary segment of the population thought I was serious and wrote letters to the newspaper. It seems there were plenty of crazy baseball fans in town who were braver than I. Darryl was right. I was too much of a coward to admit I was serious.

At any rate, I gave Darryl a lively topic for his afternoon radio show. WGCL is an AM station with an all-talk format. My friend, Darryl Robinson, hosted the afternoon show. Although he was in his thirties, he could easily pass for a grad student. Radio was a part-time gig for him. His real job was teaching speech communications at Indiana University. He looked the young professor part, sporting a shaved head and wearing glasses with round wire rims.

I had perfected the small-town reporter look: short blonde hair, average build, with a pencil usually tucked behind my right ear. A golf shirt and khakis were my summer uniform of choice.

Darryl and I had been friends since the second grade. That was when my parents had moved from Indianapolis to Bloomington. My father was born there and wanted me to grow up near my grandparents. Darryl and I had gone to Indiana University and took jobs locally when we graduated. He was the responsible one: married with two kids. I was the irresponsible one: single with a dead goldfish.

Jesse signaled to us that the commercial break was ending. In a separate booth, Kristy Parker finished reading the news and weather. Darryl thanked her and returned to the previous caller's question. "We're talking right now to Dan from Bloomington. Before the break, Dan said he would invest in a team if this was a serious effort. Dan, do you have any more to add?"

"Thanks for taking my call, Darryl. I just want to know, if this effort is for real, how can I get involved? It's always been my dream to be the owner of a pro sports franchise."

"Well, Dan, I'm going to let our in-studio guest answer that."

What a goon. He knew I had no idea how to answer that question. "Dan, I think it's premature to start sending in money. We would need to form a corporation, set up a board of directors, and do a lot of other things to convince Major League Baseball that we are a serious competitor for the Dodgers franchise."

Darryl thanked him for his question and moved on to the next caller. All the while he was laughing at me. "We're now talking to Ray on line two. What's your question, Ray?"

"Well, Darryl, I just think you need to stop having these marijuana-smoking, left-wing nuts on your show. Only a fool would think the city of Bloomington could buy a Major League Baseball team. Indianapolis only has a Triple-A franchise and they have a population of about eight hundred thousand. We have only about sixty thousand."

"Well, Ray, I've never heard Andy Bennett espouse any political leanings, so I wouldn't be inclined to label him a right-wing or a left-wing nut," Darryl said.

Apparently I was an independent nut.

Darryl made the L-shaped loser sign towards me and grinned. I grabbed a small ice cube and tossed it at him, just missing his head. Jesse scowled at both of us.

Darryl continued. "He is, however, convinced that we can pool our cash and buy the Dodgers. Next caller."

I mouthed, "No, I'm not," and threw another ice cube. Jesse took my glass. It's a sad state of affairs when two men in their thirties need to be chastised by an eighteen-year-old with acne and social studies homework.

I wrote "Darryl is a 'mic' monkey" on a piece of paper and held it up to the news booth window. Kristy, the news reporter, rolled her pretty brown eyes and kept on working. She was too serious, I thought.

"Jesse, who is on line three?"

"That would be Cecil from Smithville."

"Cecil, what do you think about today's topic?"

"Hello?" Cecil said in a slow, plodding, I-just-got-a-mechanized-plow-last-week sort of drawl.

"Cecil, are you there?"

"Darryl?"

"Yes?"

I took my headphone cable and started to strangle myself with it, prompting Jesse to smile for the first time in weeks. Kristy didn't smile.

"Darryl, I'd just like to say that the farmers of this community are not going to stand by and let this Bennett fellow chew up twenty acres of good farmland just so he can . . ."

Darryl cut him off in mid-sentence, "The stadium would be built downtown."

"Oh-umm—well, how much are tickets?" he replied after about five seconds of dead air.

"Again, let me reiterate that I was merely having fun with the idea. There would be a lot of issues that would have to be worked out to make this work." I was really backpedaling.

"Next we have David from Bloomington. What's your question, David?"

"Isn't Roland Green, the guy who owns the Mega Media Network, negotiating to buy the team? How are you going to outbid Roland Green? You can't be serious. This has to be a joke."

Moments. Life is a series of moments which punctuate the mundane, the common, and the routine. This was a *moment*. It was absurd. A small town of sixty thousand mostly middle-class people couldn't possibly outbid a billionaire media mogul. However, never underestimate a college town. College towns have liberal, radical thinkers. College towns have entrepreneurs and rich alumni. College towns have lots of crazy people with copious amounts of free time. It was because of this eclectic mix of people that this crazy ride got started. The anti-corporate people wanted to fight Roland Green. The entrepreneurs thought there was a dollar to be made. The crazy people just wanted something to do. The baseball fans wanted to chase a dream. And the twelve-year-old boys masquerading as adults wanted to see if you could really wish upon a star.

Bloomington is a community of ultraliberals and ultra-conservatives and everything in between. So when Dave from Bloomington asked "How are you going to outbid Roland Green?" he was really challenging a community.

I started to say again that it was a joke. But the air in my throat lingered for a moment. Adrenaline made me sit up straight. Why not? Why shouldn't we try? The skeptic in my brain took a leave of absence.

"We'll find a way, Dave! We'll raise the money. We'll start a massive campaign. If we have to, we'll recruit investors from all over the state of Indiana. Baseball is America's game, and what town is more American than Bloomington, Indiana? We'll galvanize this city and we'll buy the Dodgers."

When did the televangelist get here? Who was in my headphones preaching the gospel of baseball to the unwashed masses? Sweet Moses, it was me. I was possessed.

Darryl was laughing out loud, on the air. Jesse, being the only one resembling an adult in the room, cut to commercial. Darryl flipped a piece of ice at me, hitting the news booth window. Kristy jumped and spilled her coffee. She began dropping four-letter bombs from the shelter of her news booth. Due to the soundproof properties of the room, Jesse was spared the expletive chorus. Realizing that he had failed to disarm both of us, Jesse took Darryl's glass.

The phone lines lit up and reflected off the studio ceiling. Clouds that kept the station in shadow throughout the day suddenly parted. Light poured into the small windows that overlooked the street below and lit up the octagon-shaped console. That afternoon a moment of illumination occurred in the downtown AM radio station. There just might be enough people in Bloomington who believed in this idea. There might be enough people willing to put their own money on the line to chase this dream. There might be a lot of people angry at me if this didn't work. One thing was certain—it wasn't going to be just another boring summer in Bloomington.

TWO

Mocha Monoxide

(Money Raised: $200)
Sent in by Cecil from Smithville

"Baseball is a game where a curve is an optical illusion, a screwball can be a pitch or a person, stealing is legal and you can spit anywhere you like except in the umpire's eye or on the ball."

~ *Jim Murray*

"WHAT ARE YOU TEACHING FALL SEMESTER?"

"Apathy," Darryl replied, with little regard for my question.

"Seriously, what are you teaching?"

"Speech."

"Speech?"

"Yeah, speech."

"Morning class?"

"Yes."

"Those kids are screwed."

I was driving my Beirut-inspired Chevy Malibu north on Walnut Street. It was maroon with what I like to refer to as custom sport ripples down one side. Sport ripples sound more exotic than telling people I had hit a post, scraping and denting most of the passenger side of the car. It was a wonderful car if you didn't go in for things like air conditioning, stereo systems, and working windshield wipers.

Gracing the faded red cloth interior next to me was Darryl. In the back seat were my friends Klondike and Pete. Pete had arranged this trip to Ladyman's Diner the night before. He owned a movie theatre and a restaurant in town. Ten years older than Darryl and me, he had invented a special type of heart catheter when he was in his early thirties. Then he sold the company and the patents for millions of dollars. But like so many Southern Indiana millionaires, it was hard to tell him from the average Freddys.

The Four Freddys were what we called each other. A Freddy is a catch-all word for us, sometimes used as an insult and sometimes as a term of belonging. At any rate, the Four Freddys were hungry for breakfast. And a couple of the Freddys wanted to talk business.

We turned right onto Fourth Street and made a quick left into a parking lot. The lot was bordered on the north and west by the backs of several hundred-year-old buildings. Alleys divided the rows of buildings to give access to the storefront sides of the shops and restaurants. To the east and south were Lincoln and Fourth streets, respectively. The southeast corner of the parking lot doubled as a mini-hub for the city bus lines.

We parked in a space close to the buses and the north side row of buildings. On the storefront side of the buildings was Kirkwood Avenue. Kirkwood was the heart and soul of Bloomington; six blocks that run east-west from Indiana University's campus to the downtown square. It continued west of the Square for another couple of miles, but those six blocks were where everything happened in town. That's where the freaks came out to play. Business deals were done at The Uptown or the Diner. Protest marches, Fourth of July parades, funerals, weddings, all were threaded together in the fabric of Kirkwood. When Indiana University won national championships in basketball, this was where people came to party. It was the hub of the city. It was where we hatched the scheme.

From the parking lot behind the buildings, it was difficult to tell which business was which, except for the Diner. Noxious gases emitted from its dumpster. Refuse blended with grease to form an impenetrable wall to the left. However, you had to go left to get to the alley. To the right, bus fumes from Lincoln Street and the city bus terminal were mixing with fresh brewed coffee aroma from the Diner. Our options were mocha-monoxide or greasy bio-funk. I chose mocha-monoxide. It got me out in the sun and on the dry sidewalk.

Darryl walked ahead of me on the Lincoln Street sidewalk. We passed by a line of fifteen people waiting for the plasma clinic to open. Next to the clinic on the Lincoln Street side of the building was a shoe repair store that wrapped around to the Kirkwood Avenue side.

Pete followed Klondike towards the alley, finding it still damp from an overnight rain. The tall brick buildings kept the alley cool and wet, wet enough to cause Klondike to slip and fall only inches from the bio-funk dumpster.

I, on the other hand, fared worse. Just as I came around the corner, a maroon custom van barreled down Lincoln Avenue. The driver, a Neanderthal I call The Wolf, drove through a puddle doing forty miles per hour. The mud hit me doing eighty-five miles per hour. I saw The Wolf laughing in the reflection of his side mirror. I hated The Wolf.

The Wolf was a self-important blow-hard of a man. He was an attorney—reason enough for loathing—with a stranglehold on nastiness. I once reported that his son went hitless in a Little League All-Star game. He tried to sue the paper for libel. Apparently, I had failed to mention that he made a "spectacular catch in the outfield." The only thing spectacular about it was that he never stopped picking his nose when he raised his glove for the catch. His poor mother didn't know whether to be embarrassed about the nose-picking or proud that he could multitask.

He was also mad that I didn't mention that his son scored the winning run. Technically he was right. I did fail to mention it—on purpose. I was trying to save the kid some long-term teasing and embarrassment by not detailing how the run was scored. With the game tied, he was hit by a pitch in the groin. The next batter hit a home run. In the history of baseball, no runner has ever taken longer to get from first base to home plate than The Wolf's son. He did this sort of painful looking waddle that took an eternity to complete. I couldn't. I wouldn't. The kid could have been scarred for life. Then again, he was The Wolf's son. Where would his psyche squeeze in another scar? Anyway, that started a long-running feud between The Wolf and me. Today's well-aimed mud bath had given The Wolf the lead.

Klondike and I met at the door of the Diner, looked each other over and shook our heads. Someone once said, "Each man must find his own path." I'm pretty sure this is not what they had in mind, but still, here we were—two wet, smelly men who took different paths to the same destination.

As we entered the diner, my worst fear was realized. Penny was working. She was in her late twenties, cute, with a pretty smile. I always made eye contact when she was working. Now, I wanted to crawl back through the mail slot. I stood behind Klondike and Darryl. She smiled and waved us over towards a booth on the right.

Klondike, of course, bolted for the booth, without as much as a warning. There I stood with mud from my neck to my thighs. She looked me up and down, and then suppressed a giggle, causing her to snort. "I'll be right back." She returned with a towel and tossed it at me. "I heard you on the radio," she said.

"Thanks," I said. "What did you think?"

"I think you're crazy. But I have to admit you have the town stirred up. There isn't a table in here that isn't talking about it."

"Maybe they're stirred up because it's a good idea."

"No, it's crazy. You're just lucky to be living at the epicenter of crazy. It sort of clouds their judgment."

Penny took our orders and scurried off to the kitchen. I'll just eat my last meal and die, I thought. She thinks I'm a loser. A steak knife. Yeah, that's it. I'll take a steak knife and cut my wrists. No good. Klondike would pass out. I can't have that on my conscience. I'll do it in private later on tonight.

Sitting around me were my three best friends and the three best reasons I could offer for *not* going into business and certainly not trying to buy a baseball team. Darryl and I had no business background. Pete and Klondike were both businessmen, but they were from opposite ends of the spectrum. Everything Pete touched seemed to turn to gold. Klondike, on the other hand, often made money in spite of himself.

Klondike, a.k.a. Frank Lopilato, ran a small hotel in town, pitched for our softball team, and originally was from the East Coast. A short, funny-looking man, Klondike was a cross between Barney Fife and Michael Corleone. He was loyal, generous, and always coming up with a crazy marketing idea. That's how he got his nickname: Klondike. One day he had the kind of idea that you wish his wife had been around to talk him out of—or at least convince him to get counseling. "Every hotel is putting mints on the pillows at night," he said. "It's been done to death. I'm going to make people remember the Bloomington Oaks Hotel. My guests are going to come home to ice cream bars on their pillows."

So Frank put Klondike bars on all the guests' pillows. Somewhere around nine-thirty that night, the calls started to flood the front desk. One lady slid into bed without turning on the light. She still sees a therapist. Another guest's dog had been loose in his room. The otherwise docile collie vomited in seven places. Although the man's open suitcase saw most of the action, hotel workers to this day can't explain the splatters on the window. It was as if the dog was somehow trying to signal the wedding reception down by the pool.

Anyway, that's how he earned the moniker. For the most part, he was a successful businessman. Now and then, though, he went off on one of those wild tangents, and you wondered how he ever made a nickel.

Penny returned with our breakfast. "Now, judging by the amount of mud you guys tracked in here, do you want me to bring you extra napkins?"

"No, but could you take away all the silverware?" I shot back. "We'd prefer to eat with our hands."

Penny laughed and walked away. Then Pete threw out the first pitch.

"I'm ready to do it," he said. "I'm throwing in a million bucks of my own money to get the ball rolling."

"What ball rolling?" I asked.

"The baseball rolling. As in the Dodgers. Hello, I'm talking about us buying the Dodgers. I figured I would be the president; Klondike can be vice president or marketing director—"

In unison everyone turned to Klondike and said, "No ice cream."

Pete continued, "Andy, you could be the media relations director."

"Why do you get to be president?" Klondike asked.

Before he got the chance to answer, Chris Moeller, the deputy mayor, interrupted us.

It wasn't until he did that I noticed the other people in the diner. They were all looking at us. Some were whispering. Some waved their arms and talked loudly, pointing at us like animals at the zoo. Penny was right. Every table and booth was talking about the Dodgers and looking at us. In that moment, I realized this thing was alive. It was bigger than us. People had actually read the column and tuned in to the radio show. They might really want to do this. A crazy idea, born out of a need to fill my weekly requirement of nouns colliding with verbs, was about to change this town forever.

Was I reluctantly going along with this idea? Or was there a place deep inside me that wanted this more than anything? The twelve-year-old was still unsure.

"Mr. Moeller, what can we do for you?"

"What can you do for me? What can I do for you? By the way, call me Chris."

He said it in a way that made me think I was about to be sold a timeshare in Myrtle Beach.

"The mayor is behind you guys one hundred percent. He got the letter from Pete this morning and he loves the idea."

All heads turned to Pete.

"What? I just sort of greased the pump a little!"

"And what sort of grease did you use on the pump?" I asked.

"The mayor is hardly a pump," Chris said.

"Butt out, Deputy Pump," I said. What did you do, Pete?"

"I told the mayor we really would name the stadium after him."

"What?" I said.

"And I told him that the four of us were forming a corporation and would start selling shares."

"What?" Klondike and I, in unison.

"And I said we could raise the money by the end of September."

"What?" Klondike, Darryl, and I.

"Are you crazy?" I said. "This community can't raise that sort of cash."

"We'll get outside investors. We'll sell shares to anyone who wants to invest."

"We don't know how to run a baseball team."

"We'll get somebody to help us. Look, for as long as I've known you, your dream was to bring a minor league baseball team to Bloomington. Now we're going to help you go one step better. We're going to bring the Dodgers to Bloomington. The Dodgers, man. Doesn't that get you excited?"

Pete was right. Since I was twelve, I had the dream. Since I had gone to work for the *Bloomington Daily News*, I'd been trying to sell the idea of minor league baseball in B-town to anyone who would listen. It was my dream. But there's something safe about having your dream stay a dream. Keeping it a dream keeps it in a box. People think that dreams are where the possibilities are limitless. Maybe it's the other way around. Maybe reality is where things are limitless. Reality is surprising. Reality is an adventure. Reality is the intersection of *everybody's* dreams. Now my dream was about to become a reality, and I was scared.

The deputy mayor was staring at me. Klondike and Pete were staring at me. Darryl was staring at Pete (and stealing his hash browns). Then I realized the whole room was staring at me.

Pete lowered his voice and looked me in the eye. "We can't do this without you. And that means you, buying into this one hundred percent. You are the voice of baseball in Bloomington. You've got the attention of the community. They are ready to go. They just need a cheerleader. We know how to talk business. You know how to talk baseball. We'll sell people on the investment opportunity. You sell them on visions of pennants and World Series games. Say yes, and we'll go buy a baseball team. Say no, and it's another quiet summer in B-town."

"Another quiet summer in B-town." Pete's words echoed in my mind. Every summer since I graduated from Indiana University had been quiet. They all seemed to blend into each other. I didn't have much to show for the past eight years. I had worked my way up from beat reporter to a weekly column, but there was nothing distinguishing about my career, or my life, for that matter. It was time to do something. Something big. Something that people would remember. That televangelist was back in my head.

"I'm in," I shouted. "Let's buy the Dodgers."

The entire restaurant roared with applause. Darryl stole Pete's bacon.

THREE

The Big Bad Wolf Meets the DWARVES

(Money Raised: $4,263.35)

Mostly verbal commitments except for Cecil's $200 and $3.35 from Penny who gave back her tip.

"He's so ugly, when you walked by him, your pants wrinkled. He made fly balls curve foul."

~ *Mickey Rivers, on teammate Danny Napeleon's looks*

When I arrived at work the next day, my editor told me to cover an upcoming protest by the DWARVES (Defenders of Wetlands, Animals, Rainforests, Vegetation, Ecosystems, and Swampland). "Ira, I'm a sports columnist. Why are you giving this to me?"

"Because everyone else is busy and it wouldn't hurt you to broaden yourself with something besides sports."

"Well, they're having Red Stepper tryouts at Assembly Hall tomorrow. Couldn't you broaden me with that assignment?"

"You're not covering a dance squad tryout."

"What do you have against the Red Steppers? Do you hate them because they're taller than you?"

"I don't hate the Red Steppers."

"Then let me go to the tryouts."

"No, you're covering the DWARVES. That's final."

"OK, but dancers sell papers, Ira. DWARVES don't."

I left him to ponder the financial implications of a front page cover photo devoid of Red Steppers and retreated to my office. After a quick check of my messages, I called the DWARVES to get more information.

"Thank you for calling the DWARVES," said a familiar voice. It was Maple, leader of both the DWARVES and the Bloomington Vegans. She loved trees and animals–unless, of course, you viewed humans as animals. Maple assaulted me in college when I was writing for the student newspaper. During an interview, I asked how someone who loved trees so much could eat salad with such reckless abandon. I then asked her if she heard the cry of the soybean as it was grotesquely slaughtered and converted into soymilk and other bland-tasting products. The question that got me cold-cocked with a cafeteria tray, though, was how could she yank a defenseless, naked carrot from his home, skin him with a grater, and eat him raw without so much compassion as to numb him first?

That was also when I was kicked off the student newspaper even though I was the one who was assaulted. Vegan sympathy had infiltrated the decision-making offices of the Indiana Daily Student. I was an outsider, a hated meat-eater. I had dared expose the plight of defenseless farm produce. For my crime I was banished from the student press.

"Would you like to volunteer for our concert to save the Jordan River?" Maple continued.

"The Jordan River?" I asked.

"Yes, we want to put an end to illegal dumping in one of our most treasured local waterways."

"*The* Jordan River? The one that cuts through campus. That's what you're talking about?" I was starting to lose focus because of the absurdity of what she was saying. You see, the Jordan River is one of the most inaptly named "waterways" in North America. It is not a river. It's barely a stream. The only illegal dumping being done in the Jordan River is the occasional frat guy relieving himself on the way home from a party.

"Yes, that Jordan River," she answered.

"Well, the concert sounds like one heck of a good time. And the cause is certainly worthy of your organization's efforts. However, I've called about a more immediate situation. I'm calling from the *Daily News*. Could you tell me more about the protest you have scheduled this week?"

"Which one were you inquiring about?"

"Why don't you run down all of them and I'll pick the one I'm interested in."

"OK, tonight we're protesting the use of federal land for logging operations. That will be held in Dunn Meadow. Tomorrow we are holding a sit-in at the home of an attorney who is cutting down all the trees in his yard. On Friday we're marching down Kirkwood in support of—"

I cut her off, "What was that second one again?"

"We're holding a sit-in at an attorney's home."

"Which attorney?" I asked.

"Frank Wolf."

This was too good to be true. It might even be as fun to watch as the Red Steppers, for entirely different reasons of course. "Why is he cutting down the trees in his yard?"

"We learned he is putting in a pool. This will be the first in a string of protests we are planning to keep people from installing backyard pools at the expense of the environment."

"So when is the Arborcide scheduled to take place?" I asked.

"Tomorrow afternoon at one-thirty," she answered.

The next day, I pulled into The Wolf's neighborhood and parked across the street from his house. A minute later, a photographer from the newspaper arrived. I got out of my car and told him to be ready to shoot a lot of film.

Minutes later, the DWARVES started to arrive in a parade of vintage Volkswagen vans, each complete with rust and dents and tie-dyed curtains in the windows. Some had as many as fifteen people crammed inside. They covered The Wolf's yard like ants. To the untrained eye, the DWARVES appeared to be disorganized. However, there were three distinct groups, each with their own responsibilities. The Tree DWARVES chained themselves to his trees.

The Vandal DWARVES spray-painted graffiti on his house and driveway, then formed a circle in his driveway, sat down, lit some candles and began chanting. Maple emerged from one of the vans, wearing a dingy white tunic and carrying a tambourine. Barefoot with a crown of flowers adorning her hair, she skipped and frolicked around the circle while singing and pounding her tambourine. Just as that particular song ended, the men from Truelove Tree Service arrived.

The DWARVES began a Gregorian chant that nearly caused the tree foreman to wet himself. The photographer moved in closer. The flash from his camera caused the DWARVES to stop chanting and start yelping. The yelping scared me.

The third component of the group, the Marching DWARVES, proceeded to carry signs into the street to block traffic. As the servicemen tried to unload their equipment, the Vandal DWARVES circled their trucks. With their arms locked together, they began to alternate the yelping and chanting. Three tree servicemen considered the possibility of new careers that afternoon.

The foreman was able to compose himself long enough to call The Wolf's office. That's when the real circus began. It took The Wolf only seven minutes to make it from his office to his house. Arriving with him were several Bloomington police cars and a county sheriff. The police were there because The Wolf called them en route. The sheriff was there because The Wolf was doing eighty miles per hour in a school zone.

The Wolf barreled out of his van screaming at everybody in sight. Veins in his neck bulged as he shoved DWARVES, a tree service guy, and even the photographer. When he saw me taking notes, he really lost his temper. He demanded an explanation while the deputy sheriff demanded his license and registration. The deputy threatened to cuff The Wolf, so he handed him his license and stomped back to the van for his registration.

The Bloomington police didn't act immediately; the yelping threw them off. After a brief huddle, they decided to start with the Marching DWARVES. Surprisingly, they didn't put up too much of a fight. The marchers moved from the street, onto the sidewalk, and on through the neighborhood. Unfortunately for them, countless years of marijuana smoking had left them directionally impaired. The subdivision, being rather large and having many streets and cul-de-sacs, swallowed them alive.

Meanwhile, the sheriff issued The Wolf a ticket. He could have given him a warning, inasmuch as his house was under siege. But The Wolf had many enemies. Years of burning bridges, bullying prosecutors, and frivolous lawsuits had eroded his fan base to blood relatives and the acquitted.

With a vein on his neck visibly ready to rupture, The Wolf turned his attention back to the tree foreman who refused to begin cutting. The Wolf threatened to sue Truelove Tree Service. The foreman threatened to sue The Wolf. The Vandal DWARVES began to realize that there might be safer environmental battles to fight and began to flee. The Tree DWARVES, by default, were left to answer to the police.

The Wolf screamed at the Bloomington police to arrest as many of them as possible. In all, seven DWARVES went to jail that afternoon, including Maple, who failed to flee with the Vandals. I called the police later that afternoon and was told that it took them all of about twenty minutes to make bail. A deputy told me that most of them called their parents and told them they needed money for books. I also went back to the neighborhood to look for the ten Marching DWARVES. Nobody I talked to could remember seeing them.

I took what I had and wrote a story that made the front page accompanied by many wonderful pictures of the Wolf and the DWARVES. I think the headline speaks volumes about the seriousness of the event: WOLF CALLED HOME TO REMOVE DWARVES FROM TREES. I didn't stop to think that this might make the Wolf an even bigger enemy.

FOUR

Bonnie, Maple, and Other Outstanding Citizens

(Money Raised: $62,493.35)

"Just because I'm left-handed and quotable doesn't mean I'm from another solar system."

~ *Joe Magrane*

THE FIRST PUBLIC MEETING for potential shareholders took place at the Monroe County Convention Center, just a few blocks south of the downtown square. Roughly three hundred people showed up, many dressed in Dodger blue and carrying signs.

Outside the convention center, two large groups and one lone woman were picketing. Bloomington is the epicenter of Midwest Values vs. Liberal Political Correctness. It's called the "City of Trees," and believe me, they're well-hugged. On the other side of the spectrum, the Bibles in this town are well-thumped. It's a fun town if you're chronically detached from taking a stand on anything. If so, you can sit back and watch the two sides square off on the issue du jour. You can be sure that any idea will be met by the sign-carrying faithful from one end of the political spectrum to the other. Having your idea, plan, or project protested in Bloomington is the litmus test for its legitimacy. You know you're on to something when you see a group of people carrying signs. Tonight's contestants included vegans, environmentalists, and Klondike's wife.

The Bloomington Vegans were marching because of hot dogs. Apparently, the idea of pork and beef leftovers being used to produce hot dogs was particularly offensive to them. They were marching to insist that we use tofu dogs at the ballpark. I could argue that nobody had actually proven that hot dogs really are pork or beef, but I figured it was irrelevant. I don't like debating the Bloomington Vegans. They are an unhappy clan, always quick to get into a debate about culinary morality. They never seem to smile. I don't look down on them. I just feel sorry for them. I hope that there are happy vegans somewhere.

The DWARVES had turned out because of the ballpark construction. They were afraid of wetlands being destroyed, new roads being built, trees being lost, and bathing. They shouted at me as I walked by, calling me a tree murderer and an eco-traitor. One man asked if I could hear the cry of the trees. I told him if his friends could keep it down, I would try and listen. Using his middle finger, he signaled that I was number one.

It's not that I'm anti-tree or anti-green or anti-owls or whatever. It's just that the people protesting that night had made some really bad assumptions about what we were planning to do. No one had publicly mentioned anything about a site for the new stadium. Yet they just assumed we were going to start ripping down trees, desecrating wetlands, and polluting the environment. In reality, we wanted to build it downtown between the Square and IU campus on a spot that had been a public eyesore for years. No wetlands or wildlife were in danger, unless you included the termites and cockroaches that inhabited some of the old buildings we would tear down.

Klondike's wife, Bonnie, was protesting Klondike. Apparently since the morning in the diner, he had been consumed with the Dodgers. So much so, that he had missed their anniversary the night before. She carried a sign that said "Keep Frank Lopilato Off the Board of Directors." On the opposite side of the sign it read, "Ask Me Why He's a Bad Husband." No one did.

Poor Klondike. He was probably the best husband and father at the meeting. He was faithful, loving, and gentle. However, he was the beleaguered father of five girls. No man can hold up under all that estrogen. It's just not possible. Thus Klondike was more susceptible to guy things than the average male. Naturally, when guy things like this came along, he seemed to lose himself in them.

I decided to make a few notes for my column. I watched as the Vegans and the DWARVES got louder and more aggressive with the people entering the convention center. While they were taking more and more interest in who was coming, Bonnie became less aware of what was happening around her. She collided with Maple, sending the Vegan to the ground. Bonnie went pale, and then threw up. I walked over to Bonnie to see if I could help her. She took my arm and I slowly walked her into the lobby.

Nearly out of breath, she muttered, "I haven't thrown up this much since the last time I was pregnant."

"You're not pregnant again?"

She smiled, but didn't answer me.

"Does he know?"

"Not yet."

"Hope it's a boy," I said.

She went into the ladies' room to compose herself. I waited around to make sure she was all right. Inside the convention center a mass of people filled the lobby and adjoining hallways. The main auditorium was upstairs, so a steady stream of people were either walking up the stairs or riding the adjacent escalators.

Bonnie emerged from the ladies' room looking very pale. I accompanied her up the escalator and walked with her to the back row of the auditorium. Sections of white folding chairs were already filled with excited future franchise owners.

Long green curtains flanked the room on either side. The chairs faced a stage on which a podium and a half circle of padded chairs had been placed. Those chairs were empty, but numerous people were walking on and off the stage.

Bonnie assured me she was OK and I turned back towards the aisle. Across the aisle at the end of the row sat a woman in a business suit. She tossed a wave of brown hair over her shoulder so she could continue thumbing through her open brief case. As she did, it exposed her face and gave me a glimpse of her eyes.

What was my name? Why were all these people here? I'm not really sure how long I stood there staring at her. I'm sure she never noticed me. I just know that I was jelly. I was jelly with amnesia. I was so jelly that I didn't hear Bonnie vomiting, again.

"Andy!"

"What?"

"Andy!"

"What?"

"It's time to take the plunge."

"You're right. I'll ask her to marry me."

"What are you talking about?"

Darryl was standing in front of me now. I couldn't see her. The spell was broken. "What are *you* talking about?"

"It's time to start the meeting. Who are you going to ask to marry you?"

I shoved him aside, pointed towards her seat and said, "Her." She was gone. Her briefcase was there, but she was nowhere in sight. He gave me a strange look and started walking to the front of the room. I looked for her for a couple more minutes, and then slowly made my way up front to join Klondike, Darryl, and Pete.

Pete called the meeting to order and then introduced the rest of us. "Ladies and gentlemen, we have called this meeting to inform you of our intent to form a corporation. The sole purpose of this corporation will be to purchase the Los Angeles

Dodgers and move them to Bloomington, Indiana. We will make stock available to anyone wishing to purchase shares.

"Shares will go on sale Monday. Our headquarters will be on the north side of the Square, next to Stoute's Music Store. The initial management team will consist of myself as president and Mr. Frank Lopilato as vice president. A treasurer/secretary will be named shortly. Serving as marketing and communications directors will be the team of Darryl Robinson and Andy Bennett."

Darryl and I didn't have lots of cash to invest like Pete and Klondike, so we weren't on the board of directors. But our day jobs allowed us the flexibility to be involved, and Pete and Klondike treated us as equals when it came to decision-making.

Before Pete could continue, a guy in the front row yelled, "How come you get to be president? It seems we should vote on it!"

Pete waited through some applause and other comments and then answered. "We are the initial investors. I am investing nearly one million dollars of my own money and Mr. Klondike—I mean, Mr. Lopilato—has invested over five hundred thousand dollars."

Bonnie vomited again.

He continued. "We are taking the initial risk and we're going to steer this project. We're inviting you to invest along with us and to trust our vision. If we succeed in purchasing the team, there will be annual meetings of the shareholders and you can vote us out if you'd like. But for starters, this is the team that is going to run the show."

That answer must have been OK for Front Row Guy because I could see him nodding his head in agreement. From way in the back, I could see Bonnie being helped out again. She was shaking her fist towards her husband.

No one else seemed to want to challenge Pete's explanation, so he continued. "With the backing of our mayor, who will speak in a moment, we will form a task force to study potential sites for a new ballpark. We anticipate that the Dodgers will continue to play in Los Angeles as we construct a world-class baseball stadium here in Southern Indiana. When it is completed, we will move the team to Bloomington. Now, let's hear from Mayor Gomez."

Mayor Gomez talked about baseball and voting and sending a manned mission to Mars for all I know. I wasn't paying a bit of attention. Somewhere in the crowd was the woman who turned me to jelly. She wasn't sitting in the row I first saw her in. Where was she? I kept leaning to my right to try to see around Front Row Guy. He must have been about six foot seven. I leaned so far that my head was touching Klondike's shoulder. He elbowed me in the gut. I made a sound that distracted the mayor, causing him to shoot a quick glance back at us. I hoped she didn't see that.

When the mayor finished, talk turned to the name of the corporation. Pete had decided to let the attendees suggest ideas.

"Let's call it 'the Bloomington Baseball Corporation,'" someone shouted from the back of the room.

"No, I like 'Dodger Baseball Midwest,'" yelled another.

"I like 'Dodger Ball.'"

"No, no, that sounds too much like dodge ball."

I yawned through about a dozen names until Darryl said, "What about 'Trolley Dodgers, Inc.'? They were originally called the Trolley Dodgers. We can rename them when we move them to Bloomington."

Darryl was right; they really were once called the Trolley Dodgers. Before that, they had a string of odd names that I was glad nobody suggested. One glaring example: the Bridegrooms. They played under that name in 1888 because seven players got married within a few months of each other. A year later sportswriters dubbed them the Superbas after a popular vaudeville act of the same name. They remained the Superbas for over twenty years until fans and the press labeled them the Trolley Dodgers because of the complex maze of trolley lines in turn-of-the-century Brooklyn.

For Brooklyn, the trolleys represented progress. It was an industrialized, working-class, cultural melting pot. Trolleys carried people night and day to job and home. Trolleys carried dreamers, while the other dreamers darted in between them. They were American dreamers. Trolleys carried workers, while other workers marched around them. The jobs to which they went offered a slice of the American dream to immigrants, sons of immigrants, and grandsons of immigrants. The homes they returned to reminded them of the opportunity America had to offer. Although by today's standards we might think they led poor, dreary lives, compared to the lifestyles they left behind, they were living like royalty.

And the kings of Brooklyn were the Dodgers. In those days players weren't millionaires. In those days the center fielder during the summer might be the short order cook at the diner during the winter. The players lived in the towns where they played. They worked with the regular folks during the off-season.

They kept the name Trolley Dodgers for only three seasons. For the next seventeen years they were known as the Robins—for reasons that I'm sure involved grain alcohol and a lost bet. In 1932, they became the Dodgers and have been ever since. Throughout their early history, they played in the shadows of New York's Giants and Yankees. Both teams had won world championships. But in Brooklyn, a World Series title was the trolley they could never seem to catch.

In 1944, the Dodgers' fortunes would change for the worst and the best. Three businessmen purchased twenty-five percent of the franchise. Under their leadership, the Dodgers would enjoy their most prosperous years. However, this would also be the ownership group that would break the hearts of Brooklyn fans by moving the team to Los Angeles in 1957.

Still, the people of Brooklyn did get one chance to dance between the trolleys. On October 4, 1955, the Dodgers finally won the World Series. After losing the first two games of the series to the Yankees, pitcher Johnny Podres shut down the

Yankee hitters in game three. The Dodgers then won two of the next three to force a game seven. Podres again pitched a brilliant game and the hated New York Yankees, Brooklyn's biggest rival, were defeated. Podres was so popular in the Latin community abroad that a parade was held in his and the Dodgers' honor on St. Thomas Island.

The Dodgers were involved in two of the biggest stories in the history of the game. The first was the signing of Jackie Robinson. For years, black baseball players were denied the opportunity to compete with white and Latin ballplayers. The Dodgers made history when Jackie Robinson took the field wearing Dodger blue. Jackie opened the doors for other black baseball players and helped bring a World Series to Brooklyn.

The second great controversy came when the Dodgers moved west. Just when the Pacific Coast League thought they had a chance to become the third major league, the Dodgers and subsequently the Giants moved to California. Forty years later, we were trying to pull off our own Dodger controversy. Changing the name would be controversial throughout the baseball world. But tonight we just had to concern ourselves with the citizens of Bloomington.

Darryl's comment set off a wave of discussion from the front to the back of the room. The name seemed to capture everyone's imagination. I thought about it for a while. Should I point out that Bloomington doesn't have trolleys? I didn't have to.

From the back of the room came a shout. "But we don't have trolleys."

From the middle came, "Yeah, we don't have a one."

Front Row Guy said, "Uh, he's right. We ain't got any."

"But we could get one," shouted the deputy mayor.

Vernon Whip, city councilman and outstanding citizen, said, "We could get rid of all the buses and replace them with trolleys. But have you considered changing the team's name to 'the Chipmunks'?"

"Uh, he's right. We could get rid of all the buses," said Front Row Guy. Then a delayed reaction hit him. "Did you say 'chipmunks'?"

"Tell Front Row Guy to shut up," I told Pete.

"He's Mrs. Mayor's nephew."

"Of course he is."

After some more discussion, the name Trolley Dodgers, Inc., was agreed upon. We knew there was a lot of excitement in the community, but how many of these people would show up next Monday and plop down their money on a team? For the most part, these weren't rich people. They were the same people riding trolleys in Brooklyn—working-class dreamers. It was going to take a lot of them to make this work. It was also going to take a few angels with deep pockets.

FIVE

Dodger Pink

(Money Raised: $1,595,463.35)

"I ain't ever had a job. I just always played baseball."
~ *Leroy Robert "Satchel" Paige*

THE NEXT DAY, THE BOARD of directors held a special meeting for potential six-figure investors. They also were doing interviews for an interim general manager's position. My editor, Ira, let me cover the meeting, but I didn't expect much news to happen. I was mostly there to goof off and help sell the idea to potential investors.

A number of Bloomington's wealthiest men and women came to the meeting. However, most of the town's financial elite had chosen to stay away. We were still viewed by many in the community as chasing a pipe dream. The turnout worried me. We had a lot of money to raise, and this group wasn't up to the challenge.

The meeting was just about to begin, so I got up to close the door. As I was pulling the door shut, someone grabbed it from the other side.

"Excuse me," a woman's voice called out. I opened the door to a familiar face. Deep brown eyes and olive skin suggested a Latin ancestry. She wore a black business suit with a pink blouse underneath her jacket. Those eyes! I recognized those eyes. Then it hit me. She was the woman from the shareholders meeting—the one who had turned me to jelly.

"Am I too late?"

I couldn't speak. I had swallowed my gum. All I could do was shake my head and step out of the doorway so she could enter the room. She smiled at me and walked confidently into the meeting. I was baffled. Was she one of the high rollers? Was she a candidate for general manager? Was she single?

Pete made a few opening remarks and then asked the GM candidates to follow him into the hall. The woman stood up, along with four other hopefuls, and followed Pete into the hall. I was curious, so I trailed behind them. Pete explained to them that a panel of three people would interview them individually. He asked that they remain until the final interview, because one or more might be called back in for follow-up questions.

A banquet room was being used for the interviews. All the small rooms in the convention center were occupied. The panel consisted of Pete, Klondike and Darryl. Pete and Klondike represented the board. Darryl was there to evaluate the communications skills of the candidates. The conference room was set up with the three interviewers sitting at a table facing the door and the applicant. Since the room was so big and the applicant was sitting in the middle of the room facing the panel, I was able to slip in the back and listen undetected.

Pete, Klondike and Darryl each would admit that the furthest thing from their minds was to hire a woman as general manager. Baseball had zero female general managers. Baseball front offices had few women, period. Add to that, many people in Bloomington felt that the idea of hiring a new GM before the team was purchased was just plain silly. Others felt that we should retain the Dodgers' current general manager. But the majority of early shareholders felt that we should have as many locals in the front office as possible.

She was the first to be ushered into the room. Before the door shut behind her, I slid in and sat down against the wall.

As she talked, I slowly moved to an angle where I could see the side of her face and some of her expressions, yet still remain out of her line of sight.

"My name is Kathryn Ketner. You can call me Kate."

"It says in your resumé that you're a Mary Kay National Sales Director," Pete said. "Tell us about that."

Kate smiled and I could tell by the look on her face that her business was something she enjoyed talking about. "After high school I opted to get married instead of going to college. But less than a year later I found myself without a career and facing a divorce. That's when I joined Mary Kay and never looked back. I earned enough money to enroll at Indiana University and pursue a degree in business.

"As you can see, a few years later I added a master's degree in finance. Since then, through shrewd investments and my successful Mary Kay business, I have managed to build a sizeable nest egg. Not only am I seeking this position, but I am prepared to invest $250,000 in the team."

Just when Klondike asked her why she wanted to be general manager of a baseball team, my pager went off. I had to check in with the paper, so I missed the rest of her interview. Why *did* she want to be general manager?

When I returned, she was already waiting in the hallway. I mustered up the courage to introduce myself. "Hi, I'm Andy Bennett, from the *Bloomington Daily News*."

"Hi," she reached out to shake my hand. "I'm Kathryn Ketner. You can call me Kate."

"How did your interview go?"

"It went pretty well."

"You realize, if hired, you would become the first woman general manager in baseball history—sort of like Jackie Robinson with better legs?" I winced at my own comment. How did that idiotic statement come out of my mouth?

She laughed. "I guess I never thought of it that way. However, I would never compare myself to Jackie Robinson. It took much more courage for him to become the first black player in the major leagues than for me to be the first female general manager."

Her statement revealed much more than some passing knowledge of the game's history. She was poised and could answer tough questions in a way that reflected positively on an organization. She would have no trouble handling a press conference.

Although just looking at her still made me jelly, I found that she was very easy to talk to. In fact, I was amazed when I realized that they had finished with the last candidate and I had missed all of the interviews but hers. After about another twenty minutes, during which they deliberated about the candidates, the Freddys called me into the room.

"What happened to you?" Darryl asked.

"I was talking to the new GM."

"Who?" Pete said.

"Kate."

"You were supposed to listen to all of them. You blew off the other interviews." Klondike rolled his eyes.

"I didn't need to hear them. She's the one."

"The one you're obsessed with or the one who should be GM?"

"Yes."

"Yes to which?"

"Both. Guys, she's poised, polished and can handle herself in an interview. She's beautiful, which never hurts at a press conference, and she can raise tons of money through her Mary Kay network. Think of all the boyfriends and husbands of Mary Kay consultants who would want to own a few shares of a baseball team. Please."

I held my hands like I was praying. Then I knelt in front of them. "Do this for me and I will do anything."

"Watch my kids tonight," Klondike said.

"And clean my house," Pete added.

Darryl thought for a few seconds. "Give me your Mickey Mantle rookie card."

"You're a bunch of Freddys," I told them.

"She's way out of your league anyway," Klondike shot back.

They all nodded in agreement.

"We had already decided we were going to hire her," said Pete. "We just wanted to see you beg. Tell her to come back in."

Kate was sitting in the hallway when I came out. The other candidates were pacing back and forth. I motioned for her to come back into the room.

Pete began, "Have a seat, Ms. Ketner. I'm pleased to inform you that we would like to offer you the position. As we mentioned in the interview round, if we are successful in purchasing the team, you will be required to move to Los Angeles in the interim. After having some time to think about it, are you still willing to relocate?"

"Yes I am," she answered.

"Good," Pete said. "The transition team will probably leave in October, just after the completion of the World Series."

Klondike asked, "You mentioned in the earlier interview that you would continue with Mary Kay and work around our schedule. How soon will you be able to start?"

"Now," she said. Then she surprised everyone by standing up and announcing, "Let's get to work."

"What do you mean?" Pete asked.

"You've got twenty-five high rollers in the other room, don't you?"

"Yes."

"Well, let's go sell them some stock in our company."

The guys just nodded in agreement and followed Kate back to the big room. Pete introduced the board and the prospective investors to their new general manager. She worked magic in that room. Donors were filling out pledge cards as fast as they could write. In forty-five minutes, she nearly doubled our fundraising. When the board tallied up the pledges, they were stunned.

"Can you believe how much we raised today? $2.3 million dollars," Pete yelled. "Maybe she should be CEO."

Klondike's gum dropped out of his mouth. "Maybe," was all he could say.

Kate showed a little crack in her business-like exterior. She smiled and took a bow before her new adoring fans. "Not bad for the first day on the job," she said.

SIX

Exposing Ourselves

(Money Raised: $3,900,003.35)

A special thanks to City Councilman Vernon Whip for the $300 in Sacagawea Dollar coins.

"I'm not an athlete. I'm a professional baseball player."
~ *John Kruk*

KATE AND PETE CONVINCED the convention center director to allow us to use the facility for a press conference the following Monday. Meanwhile, over the weekend, we prepared the new home of Trolley Dodgers, Inc.

We opened up an office on the north side of the Square. The building owner traded us shares for rent, so we didn't have any upfront costs. People pitched in on a Saturday to decorate the office. It had a glass front door and large glass display windows on either side. We painted the door and window frames Dodger blue. The inside walls were painted white. Large team logos were painted on the east wall. A six-foot-tall "B" with a script tail was painted near the entrance on the west wall.

Shareholders brought their own baseball memorabilia to hang on the walls. It took a little convincing, but we allowed Kate's friends to paint one of the logos Dodger blue with a Mary Kay pink outline. The outline was done in such a way that it appeared the word "Trolley Dodgers" had been traced in pink neon. I had to admit it looked pretty good.

The space was a long narrow storefront, shaped like a rectangle. In the back were a bathroom and a storage closet. A back door led to a brick-paved alley used for deliveries to each of the businesses on the north side of the downtown square. In the front of the office were several desks. Towards the back of the room we set up a conference table and chairs, separated by a temporary partition. None of the furniture matched. All of it was second-hand stuff people brought from their homes.

By the end of the day, everyone involved in the office project was exhausted. As people started to file out, I decided to risk asking Kate to have dinner with me. I figured that she was too worn out to be thinking clearly and that might increase my chances of success.

"Do you eat meat?" I began. (I was tired too.)

"All the time."

"Have you ever eaten at Janko's Little Zagreb?"

"Absolutely."

"Have you ever been there with a single male reporter?"

"Never."

She wasn't making this very easy. "Have you ever *considered* going there with a single male reporter?"

"That depends. What does he write about?"

"Sports."

"Hmm. I don't know. There's more to life than sports."

"He's written about other things before."

"Has he ever written about make-up?"

"I don't think so."

"I'd say his chances aren't very good."

"Don't consider it dinner. Consider it background for a future story about make-up."

"Would he wash the blue paint off his face?"

"His face and anywhere else he might have blue paint."

"That's way too much information. I'll tell you what; I'll meet you for lunch next week. We can go downtown to the Trojan Horse and make it a Trolley Dodgers business meeting."

"Why can't we go to Janko's?"

"For starters, they're not open for lunch. Second, you have to earn the right to take me to Janko's."

"OK, I'll settle for lunch. Pick me up at the newspaper Tuesday at eleven-thirty."

"Why do I have to pick you up?"

"You have to earn the right to ride in my car."

"It's a piece of crap."

"How dare you slander the Scarlet Cricket. I'll see you in court for that remark."

"Your car is named the Scarlet Cricket?"

"Yes."

"You are so weird."

"Like it?"

"No."

"Well, it will grow on you."

"I hope not," she said, but I saw a glimpse of a smile.

"Good luck with Monday's press conference."

"Thanks."

The media didn't necessarily descend on Bloomington when we had our first press conference. We notified everyone from ESPN to CNN, but they all thought it was a joke. Besides the local paper and news radio stations, the only out-of-town media representative was a reporter for the *Indianapolis Star*. He wasn't even covering the baseball story. He was late for the Southern Indiana Mayors' Conference held in the convention center that morning. However, when he accidentally wandered into our press conference, he got the scoop of a lifetime.

Kate led off the meeting. "Ladies and gentlemen, it is my pleasure to announce the formation of Trolley Dodgers, Inc. Trolley Dodgers, Inc. is dedicated to one purpose: purchasing the Los Angeles Dodgers and moving them to Bloomington, Indiana."

The *Indianapolis Star* reporter had been lurking near the coffee and snacks table at the back of the room. When the phrase "purchasing the Los Angeles Dodgers" came out of

Kate's mouth, he spit coffee all over a plate of chocolate chip cookies. He dropped his coffee cup, which spilled onto a veggie platter. Cauliflower looks weird soaking in coffee. He took a pen from behind his ear and furiously flipped through his spiral notepad to find a blank page. All the while, he was stumbling down the aisles of empty seats toward the front of the room. He finally crashed into a chair and started taking notes. He made such a commotion that everyone in the room briefly took notice of him. Even Kate paused for a moment and then continued.

"Starting next Monday at nine a.m., shares of Trolley Dodgers, Inc., will be available for purchase. Our goal is to raise $250 million, the asking price of the McGuire family who currently owns the Dodgers. Our major competitor in this effort is, of course, Roland Green, owner of the Mega Media empire."

The Star reporter made a sort of snorting sound. I couldn't tell if he was laughing or choking. Probably both. Kate patiently waited for him to compose himself, then continued.

"We must raise this money by the end of August or show that we have the ability to raise it. We have assembled a staff and board of directors who I am confident will help us achieve this goal. In the last two weeks, we already have commitments of over eight million dollars."

Then Kate opened the floor for questions. Mr. *Indianapolis Star* nearly wet himself trying to get her attention. He didn't seem to realize that there were only three reporters in the room. Everyone else at the meeting was a shareholder.

"Miss—um—I didn't get your name at the start of the press conference."

"That's because you weren't here at the start of the press conference." Kate sounded like Bob Knight. "My name is Kathryn Ketner. I am the interim general manager of Trolley Dodgers, Inc."

"Ms. Ketner, does Major League Baseball know you are attempting to buy the Dodgers?"

"Yes, we sent them a registered letter on Tuesday. We have yet to hear back from them. Your question." She pointed to the *Bloomington Daily News* reporter.

"Ms. Ketner, is three months enough time to raise that kind of money?"

"We feel confident that we can raise that amount or at least enough to be taken seriously by the league. It's not necessary that we have all the money in place, but we must show we are capable of raising it."

The *Star* reporter cut her off. "What makes you think you can compete with Roland Green? He could buy the Dodgers and this entire city."

Kate didn't hesitate for even a moment before she responded. "We feel that public support will be on our side. Americans can identify with a team owned by the people. The idea has a certain type of charm that people will embrace. Americans are tired of the mega-corporations gobbling up business after business. Americans don't want to see one of their beloved sports franchises become part of a global media empire. When the Dodgers were in Brooklyn, they were the champions of the working man. Common folk identified with 'Dem Bums,' as they were affectionately referred to by their fans. We want to return the franchise to the working men and women of this country. Today everyone in America can buy stock in the Dodgers."

I swear "The Star Spangled Banner" was playing in the background at that moment. I was ready to play baseball, fight communism, give blood, or something. The board of directors gave her a standing ovation. Even the reporters were clapping.

Despite the lack of major media outlets at the press conference, it didn't take long for the story to gain national attention. The *Indianapolis Star* ran it on the front page the next day. The radio station had taped Kate's speech, which was rebroadcast in New York, L.A., and everywhere in between. Over the next three days, Kate was interviewed on *SportsCenter*, *Good Morning America*, and *The Jim Rome Show*. The entire country had its eye on Bloomington. On the following Monday, when stock officially went on sale, the telephone operators at headquarters were overwhelmed. Even though they weren't selling shares, a Merrill Lynch stock analyst reported on CNBC that they had received twenty thousand calls in one day.

On Tuesday, Major League Baseball finally made an official statement. For an entire week, the press had been hounding them to make a comment. Many sports and stock analysts were holding their breath, waiting for official word as to whether the National League would even allow us to pursue the Dodgers. The type of ownership model we were proposing was against baseball rules. In our letter to MLB, we had asked for special dispensation in regards to team ownership.

Through Pete's political connections, we had managed to get our U.S. representatives and senators to write letters to MLB on our behalf. Still, we had heard nothing from the commissioner's office, and we were starting to get worried. The league was under no legal obligation to allow such an effort to continue. They could have just come right out and said that they would not allow us to purchase the team. However, the media circus we had generated caused them to move slowly and consider their options. After the fairy-tale aspect of the story had worn thin, the media started to voice the same concerns. When they could avoid the question no more, the commissioner held a press conference from MLB headquarters in New York. Members of the local press gathered at Trolley Dodgers headquarters to watch it live.

"Today, I would like to discuss the matter of the sale of the Los Angeles Dodgers. It is the policy of Major League Baseball not to allow the sale of common stock of one of its franchises. Thus, the ownership structure being proposed by a group in Bloomington, Indiana, is not consistent with league rules and policies."

Grumbling and groaning filled the room. The commissioner continued, "However, we see a strong commitment from the parties involved and a viable business model has been presented to us by Trolley Dodgers, Inc. For these reasons, the ownership committee has voted to allow Trolley Dodgers, Inc., to compete with all other legitimate bidders for the purchase of the Los Angeles Dodgers."

Everyone in the room cheered and clapped. The commissioner continued. "The committee has stipulated that if the sale of the team by the McGuire family results in the moving of the team, the Los Angeles area will be moved to the top of the list for any future league expansion. In addition, special consideration will be given to a struggling franchise that might wish to relocate to Los Angeles."

Now we were in business. With the official OK from the league office, we were able to go after some serious investors. We needed two types of investors: everyday people who wanted to be able to say they owned a piece of a baseball team, and heavy hitters who could plop down a million or two at a time. Although we would have loved to have ownership completely comprised of the first type, we knew we couldn't survive without the latter.

The next day our board members hit the pavement. Their network of business associates and country club cronies netted us eleven six-figure investors and a couple of million dollar investors in a little over a week. Meanwhile the grassroots investors were starting to number in the tens of thousands. ESPN started running a ticker every night on *SportsCenter* that showed how much money had been raised.

For Kate's next press conference, the convention center was packed. They had to use the main room because so many media outlets had come to Bloomington to cover the story. I noticed *Indianapolis Star* Guy was on time and sitting in the front row. He had the fear of Kate in him.

SEVEN

Gomez Park, Home of Good Oral Hygiene

(Money Raised: $8,563,423.35

"A baseball club is part of the chemistry of the city. A game isn't just an athletic contest. It's a picnic, a kind of town meeting."

~ *Michael Burke*

AT THE NEXT MEETING OF the Bloomington City Council, the first item on the agenda was the matter of replacing the city buses with trolleys. Many of the city buses were ancient anyway, so replacing them was not a huge deal. However, not everyone on the council was behind the idea of bringing baseball to B-town. The leader of the opposition was Paula Sherwood. Paula looked like a fifty-year-old version of the Peanuts character Peppermint Patty. She had a well-weathered face that never bore makeup. Her hair was mostly black with streaks of grey, and cut in a bowl style reminiscent of Moe from the Three Stooges.

The trolley idea posed a unique problem for Ms. Paula; it represented environmentally friendlier mass transit, but it also represented the coming of new industry, new businesses and in general, new development. You see, there were two main schools of thought when it came to downtown Bloomington. There were those who were for development, progress, and a business-friendly climate. And there were those who wanted to turn downtown into a state park: eliminate cars, trucks, etc. This group would rather see the downtown populated by pedestrians, skateboarders and deer.

City Council Chairman Charlie Waggoner called the meeting to order. Bill Green announced the trolley motion and the chairman opened the floor for discussion. A huge crowd of people had crammed into the council chambers so I knew this was going to be a hotly debated topic.

Paula stood up. "I think this is grossly premature. We don't even know if we will have the winning bid."

"As mentioned in the reading of the proposed resolution," Chairman Waggoner replied, "only a couple of trolleys would be purchased now, and the full conversion would take place when and if the Dodgers move to Bloomington."

Then he called for a picture to be displayed on the overhead projector. The picture showed a bus designed to look like a trolley. It was Dodger blue with green and white trim.

"The design allows us to display ads on the side, space we can sell to recoup some of the cost of upkeep. Even if we don't get the team, having these trolleys running downtown routes will give an added bit of character to promote tourism. You'll notice, if you look closely, some of the design elements found in the trim match some of the design elements from Kirkwood Avenue and other recently restored corridors of our city."

After another half hour of debate, the motion was put to a vote. The council voted in favor of the new trolleys with only one member (Paula) voting against. As I got up to leave, I heard Vernon Whip make a motion to take the fish scul-pture off the Monroe County Courthouse and replace it with a chipmunk. Vernon has made the same motion at every meeting since he was elected to the city council. Every time he makes the motion, nobody seconds it. But Vernon, sporting his chipmunk tie, is undaunted. He continues to bring attention to the chipmunk in any forum he happens to find himself in. Nobody has ever had the guts to ask him why.

The next afternoon, the Dodgers' All-Star third baseman, Adam Riley, called a press conference. Rumors had been circulating for weeks that he would demand a trade if the team was sold to Bloomington. I met the rest of the gang at Trolley Dodgers headquarters to listen. It was a critical event for us. We needed to see how the rest of the world perceived our efforts. We were tuned to ESPN, which carried the press conference live.

For a few minutes before it started, ESPN played sound bytes of various baseball people reacting to our attempts to buy the team. Most of them could be summed up by their manager's reaction on *Baseball Tonight*: "Where the (ESPN bleeped him) is Bloomington, Indiana?" That quote led right into the press conference.

Riley stepped to the podium. "I have come to read a brief statement, and then I will field some questions. At the end of this season, I will exercise my option to become a free agent. This is not a reflection of my thoughts on the potential new ownership. It is, however, my desire to move back to the East Coast where I grew up."

So there it was. The first team defection. Dodger fans would blame us. Despite what he said, they would think he didn't want to move with the team. Fans across America would doubt that we could attract quality ballplayers. We needed damage control and fast.

Pete called an emergency meeting of the board and invited members of the city council and the mayor. The meeting lasted well into the night, and out of it was hatched the most extensive development scheme Bloomington has ever seen. The next day the city council met in emergency session and voted to approve it. The vote was not unanimous, but it didn't matter.

On Friday, the City of Bloomington held a press conference of its own. The plan was brilliant. Monroe Reservoir, south of town, was already the site of some very expensive homes owned by well-to-do individuals. Developers of The Pointe announced that an expanded subdivision of multi-million dollar homes would be added to the community, presumably to attract ballplayers.

The county announced upgrades to the airport with a new hangar to house private jets, presumably for players who would want to live in Chicago or one of its suburbs, and a helicopter shuttle to Carmel for players who would choose Indy's prestigious far north side (where many Colts and Pacers live). Plans for a five-star hotel were announced to accommodate the many out-of-town opposing team guests. Klondike had struck a deal to have it built on the site of his existing hotel. He stood to make a fortune.

It was also at this press conference where plans were announced for developing the neighborhood around the stadium. Shops, restaurants and bars were featured. In addition, condos and apartments would be built. The plan was ambitious, risky and downright genius.

Weekend reaction was better than we could have hoped for, turning the momentum back in our direction. A thousand new investors bought one-hundred-share blocks and Terry Hanson, the Dodgers' closer and a native of Evansville, Indiana, told reporters he would be the first to buy a home on Lake Monroe. Exactly one week from Adam Riley's announcement, our number of investors had nearly doubled. The world knew we were now serious contenders for the L.A. Dodgers.

But to truly convince Major League Baseball and the rest of the country that we were a big league town, we needed a ballpark. We needed to release plans for a place for the team to play. It had to be impressive, creative, and generate a buzz throughout the country. We needed it to be designed by a top stadium design company. Instead, we had Klondike and a local architect.

Quirks and legends. Odd dimensions and local superstitions. Design and function. These are some of the elements that separate the great ballparks in America from the mundane. The ivy in Wrigley Field, the right field warehouse at Camden Yards, and the Green Monster at Fenway are all characters in the American narrative known as baseball. Gomez Park, the new home for the Trolley Dodgers, was designed to have more character than any park in baseball history. It was character designed by Bloomington's biggest character: Klondike.

Klondike unveiled his master plan during a press conference at Trolley Dodgers headquarters. It combined the best amenities of all the current ballparks with the off-the-wall absurdity you would expect from the average Midwestern college town.

The nonsense started behind home plate. Pete and Klondike were already taking deposits on ad space, naming rights, etc. Apparently they struck a deal with a local dentist who purchased seats behind home plate. Instead of putting in regular seats, they planned to install dentist chairs. "Other dentists let you watch baseball on a television monitor while you're having your teeth cleaned," said Klondike. "At Gomez Park, you can watch *live* baseball while maintaining good oral hygiene."

I interrupted his presentation. "No pitcher is going to be able to hit the strike zone while some Freddy is getting a root canal behind home plate."

"The doctor will only drill when the opposing team is in the field," he answered.

I rolled my eyes. Klondike continued. Monroe County, being blessed with large quantities of limestone, has a great many quarries. To celebrate Bloomington's association with the limestone business, in place of a left-field fence was a twenty-five-foot-high limestone wall, opposite a makeshift quarry filled with water so people could swim. Fenway had the Green Monster; we would have Cutter's Corner.

Other features included men's urinals with field views. Right field was re-named Rowdy Field and a deal was announced to have IU fraternities and sororities fill the right-field bleachers via cheap tickets and cheap beer. Behind the Rowdy Field bleachers were a Hooters restaurant and a tattoo parlor.

As I studied the drawings they had made available to the press, I noticed a very odd feature in the stands. Just past third base, about twenty-five rows up, was a large glass window that extended from the seats to the deck above. Since Klondike had not mentioned this feature, I asked him to explain it.

"Oh, this is probably one of the most politically correct, forward-thinking, fan-sensitive features in the history of baseball. It's a bifocal magnifying window."

"It's a what?" I asked.

"It's a bifocal magnifying window for senior citizens to watch the game. No one under sixty-five will be able to purchase tickets in this section. For those seniors who love the game but have poor eyesight, this will bring them closer to the action."

I could hear the lip-smacking, salivating glee of personal injury lawyers everywhere. "Is it shatterproof? What about foul balls?"

"Hey, that's a good idea," he answered. "Let me write that down."

I wasn't sure I wanted to hear any more, but since I was there in my *Daily News* capacity, I had to ask. "Do you have any more special features we should know about?"

"Yes, at the end of the right-field line, just before Cutter's Corner, we have a section for those people who are opposed to eating meat. A special concession stand on the concourse behind those seats will carry tofu dogs and other animal-free menu items. The Bagel Company has agreed to occupy two concession stands. We will also have Greek, Tibetan, Mexican, Thai, and Canadian concession stands."

"Did you say Canadian?"

"Yes I did."

"What, may I ask, will be served at the Canadian concession stand?"

"It will feature things like back bacon, LaBatt's beer, and of course hamburgers with mayonnaise."

It was at this point that I wondered if we were taking this inclusion thing maybe a bit too far. Was there a burgeoning Canadian population in Bloomington of which I was completely unaware? Klondike continued. “I would also like to point out that Long’s Furniture Company has agreed to purchase section thirty-two down the right-field line. Instead of traditional bleachers, that section will be filled with couches and La-Z-Boys. You will also notice that beyond the center field wall, we have included a small forest consisting of several varieties of trees to celebrate the Hoosier National Forest just north of Bloomington, and to commemorate the loss of the ten DWARVES earlier this summer. It will be called the DWARVES Forest and will be open for picnics before and after games.”

“What if they turn up?” I asked.

“Who?”

“The DWARVES! They’re still just listed as missing.”

“Then we’ll change the name.”

“OK,” was all I could muster in response. At this point I was dumbfounded. This ballpark was bizarre, even by Klondike’s standards. Certainly baseball purists would shun it as a circus environment. But the more I thought about it, the more I realized it was the perfect reflection of a Midwestern college town. All of the quirks and all of the special interests were represented by Gomez Park. It would be a palace for Freddys.

EIGHT

Katarina Witt Never Complained About My Flippers

(Money Raised: $15,345,763.35)

"There comes a time in every man's life and I've had plenty of them."

~ *Casey Stengel*

MY OFFICE AT THE NEWSPAPER was a shrine to the game of baseball, with a few artifacts from other sports sprinkled in for variety. I really hadn't been working there long before I was moved out of a cube and into an office. The move had nothing to do with seniority or journalistic accomplishment. Most of the other reporters felt I was disruptive and criminally insane, and thus wanted me hidden away.

My signature quirk at the *Bloomington Daily News* was my hat collection. On any given day, I could be seen wearing a sombrero, a Roman soldier's helmet, or a pope's miter. Some days it wouldn't be a hat at all. I would don a snorkel, mask and fins. My favorite was an old Baltimore Orioles batting helmet. It was the plastic kind they used to sell at the ballpark. It was black with an orange bill and a white front panel. The white panel featured the cartoon bird mascot. Over the years some of the white paint had flaked off, but I replaced it with Wite-Out from the office.

The hats and the bizarre behavior were, of course, a ruse. My theory was that the crazier your co-workers think you are, the more likely they are to leave you alone. Most of the time, it worked.

The south wall of my office was lined with bookshelves that were starving for books. Instead of great works of literature, there were autographed pictures, autographed baseballs, and a Wheaties box with Johnny Bench on it. A few baseball reference books were included for settling trivia disputes.

Non-baseball items included boxing gloves autographed by Muhammad Ali and an autographed picture of Katarina Witt (whom I was madly in love with). Next to Katarina was a basketball autographed by Dick Vitale and an autographed picture of the Hanson brothers from the movie *Slap Shot*.

A lithograph by Bill Purdom hung on the opposite wall. Entitled "Amazing Polo Catch," it depicted Willie Mays making his signature World Series catch in center field of the Polo Grounds. Sometimes I just stared at it for hours.

On the carpet were the taped outlines of two dead bodies. When visitors came to my office, I liked to watch the tension build as they wondered what might have happened in here. Sometimes I pretended not to notice, and sometimes I made up wild stories about two nighttime cleaning workers having a passionate affair, then killing each other in my office with hand-held Dustbusters.

The paper was owned by the Douglass chain of newspapers. Occasionally, they sent a suit down from their headquarters in Minneapolis to check on us. The last time one of their corporate people came down, Ira, the managing editor, told us to clean our offices and be on our best behavior. I confess I have an unhealthy delight in making Ira sweat.

Anyway, when inspection day came, I threw a cocktail party in my office. I conned the seven-foot center from the Indiana University basketball team into dressing like Abe Lincoln and being the doorman. Inside the office were Red Steppers (IU's dance squad) serving hors d'oeuvres and drinks. They were accompanied by a performance artist reciting from *Othello* in an obscure African dialect while painting faces on ping-pong balls. Only the journalism awards on my wall saved my job that day.

On another occasion, I came to work in fatigues and a soldier's helmet. On the helmet was a white peace sign. I kept Vietnam War movies playing in my office all day. Whenever an explosion took place in the movie, I would throw debris in the hall. Boy, were people freaked out. You've never seen so many people asking to go home early in your life.

The first time Kate came to see me at work, I had been in one of my eccentric moods. On my feet were flippers. I couldn't decide between the Mexican or aquatic theme that morning, so I chose both. Had I remembered she was coming, I would have been on my best behavior. Unfortunately I thought our lunch meeting was the next day, so I was wearing a ridiculously large sombrero and a poncho.

The sombrero was so large that you couldn't see my face at all when I was sitting at my desk. The only way you could tell I was awake was from the clicking of my keyboard. I was writing a story about an upcoming race at the Bloomington Speedway when I heard someone clear their throat outside my door.

"Andy?"

I looked up slowly. I knew that voice. I didn't want her to see me like this . . . yet. I could hear her giggling. As I slowly looked up, I recognized those legs, that body, the face and the hair.

"You look ridiculous."

"It's all part of my master plan."

"Which is?"

"To keep them thinking I'm crazy while I take over."

"It's working. I think you're crazy. So, when you take over, will everyone wear sombreros?"

"Only leaders and the cool people."

"Interesting. I may regret this, but do you still want to have lunch? If the answer is yes, the sombrero stays here."

"Sure, I'd love to. But are you sure about the sombrero? Being seen with a man in a sombrero would make you the envy of all the other Mary Kay ladies."

"Maybe some other time."

"OK," I said, dejected. Then I followed her out of my office and down the hall.

"Shoes."

"What?"

"I will not have lunch with a man in flippers." She seemed angry. "Go back to your office and put on some shoes."

As I walked back to the office, she added, "Ones that are appropriate to your outfit."

When I came back, she was standing in the same place I had left her, but laughter had replaced the stern tone in her voice. "You really are crazy."

"I prefer the more politically correct term, alternatively adjusted to reality."

"You think anyone will buy that?"

"They haven't so far."

"I'm not surprised."

"Do you still want to eat at the Trojan Horse?"

"Yes, I love their gyros!"

When we arrived at the Trojan Horse, the only available booth was adjacent to The Wolf. We snarled at each other. "What's with the two of you?" Kate asked.

"We have a mutual dislike for one another," I answered. "He doesn't like reporters, and I don't like reptiles that feel the need to mingle with humans."

"Is it because he's an attorney? Are you prejudiced against lawyers?"

"No, he'd pretty much be a jerk no matter what profession he chose."

"Well, maybe if you took the time to get to know him, you'd find there is more substance underneath that tough exterior."

"Kate, have you *seen* this guy's commercials? There isn't more beneath the exterior, there's less."

"Oh, I forgot about those commercials. Yeah, you're right. He's a jerk."

The Wolf had long been known to refer to himself in the third person during his personal injury commercials. Since he had ventured into the fitness club business, the commercials were even more self absorbed. I don't know if he had heard our conversation, but at that moment, he stood up and leaned towards our booth.

"Mr. Bennett, there's a rumor going around that you were responsible for that fiasco in my yard a few weeks ago. If I find a shred of proof, I'm going to sue your pants off."

"You'd like that, wouldn't you, Frank? To see me without pants? I'm sorry, Frank, my heart belongs to another."

"You're an idiot. You know what I mean. And I hope by your heart belonging to another, you don't mean Ms. Ketner here. She's out of your league."

That riled Kate. "That's none of your business."

"Why does everyone keep telling me that?" I asked.

The Wolf said, "Because she's out of your league," at the same time Kate said, "Because I'm out of your league."

The Wolf laughed. Kate looked embarrassed. "Ouch!" I said. "Wolf, go away now. Go sue somebody." He walked towards the bathroom, mocking me all the way.

"I'm sorry," Kate said. "That probably sounded much harsher than I meant it to be."

"I'm not in your league?" I asked.

She shook her head. "It's complicated. We're from two different worlds. We run with completely different people. Besides, we're going to be co-workers. I'll be your boss."

"No dates?"

"No."

"No Janko's?"

"No."

"No holding hands when they play 'Take Me Out to the Ballgame'?"

"*No*!" She gave me the weirdest look when I mentioned "Take Me Out to the Ballgame." "But you think I'm cute?"

"Yes."

"And amusing?"

"Yes."

"And much more of an outstanding citizen than The Wolf?"

"*Yes*!" she laughed. It was a good laugh, the kind of laugh a person does when they've let their guard down a little. The laugh quickly turned to horror when The Wolf came back and collided (I believe intentionally) with the waitress, sending an entire pitcher of iced tea in my lap.

"I guess I won't have that refill on my tea," The Wolf said to the waitress.

She wheeled around and glared at him. "You did that on purpose."

"And you aren't getting a tip," he shouted back.

Before I could utter a word, he grabbed his check and slithered up to the cashier. The waitress joined Kate in piling napkins in front of me.

"I'm so sorry. I'll ask the manager to give you your lunch for free."

"It's OK," I reassured her. "I think he pushed you intentionally."

The waitress retreated to the kitchen for a towel. There is something about spending time with someone with a large tea stain on his shirt and pants that compels you to try to take the person's mind off their wetness. That's probably because you're imagining that although the surface has been blotted dry, the undergarments may indeed still be soggy. Thus Kate quickly tried to get my mind off the tea.

"Have you ever been married?"

"No."

"Ever been close?"

"Yes."

"What happened?"

"NASCAR."

"NASCAR happened?"

"Yes."

"OK, could you expand on that a little?"

"She left me for a driver."

"You got dumped for a NASCAR driver? I don't believe it."

"I did, sort of."

"What do you mean, sort of?"

"He wasn't really a driver."

"I'm confused."

"He told her he was a driver. He was actually a pit boy or something."

"OK, so you're telling me your ex-girlfriend—"

I cut her off. "Fiancé."

"Your ex-fiancé," she paused as the last word triggered something in her mind. "Wow, you were engaged? And she dumped you for a driver."

"Pit boy."

"For a pit boy, whom she thought was a driver."

"And married."

"She thought he was married?"

"No, she thought he was single, but he was married."

"Are you sure this wasn't a Springer episode?"

I looked at her and growled. "No, that was my life."

"When did this happen?" she asked.

"Two years ago. She met him at the Brickyard 400 in Indianapolis. She went to qualifications with some of her girlfriends and bumped into this guy. He convinced her that he was a backup driver. She mailed me her engagement ring from somewhere on the road to the next race. It took two weeks for her to figure out he wasn't really a driver and another two weeks before he abandoned her at the Charlotte speedway. Apparently, his wife was rejoining the entourage at the next race."

"That's so sad."

"For me or her?"

"For both of you. Although she got what she deserved. Did she come back to Bloomington?"

"Yes, she tried to get back together with me."

"How did you handle that?"

"I moved."

"Well, that was a mature response. Way to confront your problems."

"Hey, cut me a little slack."

"Why didn't you stand up to her? Tell her off? Anything?"

"It's not like I totally ran away. Her brother lived next door to me, so I had to see her all the time. She lost her apartment when she turned racecar roadie and didn't have a place to live. She showed up on my doorstep and I refused to let her stay with me. Next thing I know, she's living next door."

"OK, that I can understand. Where is she now?"

"Last I heard, she had moved to Colorado."

"Nature lover?"

"Ski groupie."

"Perfect," she said.

The waitress brought me another towel. I thanked her and tried to dry myself a little more.

"You were married before, right?"

"Yes, I was married for less than a year. I've been divorced for almost ten years now. I've spent most of my time building my business, going to school, and watching the Cubs."

"Why didn't you ever remarry?" I asked.

"I guess I never found someone who would let me live my own life, have my own dreams, pursue my ambitions. How come you never married?"

"I guess I never found someone I was sure I could make happy."

She looked puzzled by my answer.

"You see, with my ex-fiancé, I made her laugh and occasionally made her breakfast. But I ran out of ways to make her happy. It was never enough for her. She always made me feel like plan B. She was settling for me until someone better came along."

"Like Pit Boy."

"Exactly."

As we walked back to her car after lunch, I could feel iced tea running down my leg inside my pants. She gave me a towel to sit on so I wouldn't stain her seats. While riding back to my office, I posed a final question. "So, what are you looking for in a man?"

"Tall, dark, and handsome."

"That's just a cliché. Every girl says that. What are you really looking for?"

"No, actually that really *is* what I'm looking for."

I laughed. "Well I'm hitless on those criteria, so I hope you and The Wolf are very happy together." I opened her car door to get out. "Thanks for driving."

"The Wolf's a little too slimy for my taste. Besides, you haven't been sent to the minors yet. Let's just say you're still in spring training." She smiled, winked, and drove off.

As Hawk and Wimpy used to put it when they announced White Sox games together, "That was a duck snort."

NINE

Monday Night at Roxy's

(Money Raised: $18,131,523.35)

"Kids today are looking for idols, but sometimes they look too far . . . they don't have to look any farther than their home because those are the people that love you. They are the real heroes."

~ *Bobby Bonilla*

I WAS STILL FEELING GOOD about my lunch with Kate when I left work that afternoon. After cutting across town to the west side of Bloomington, I made my way to a familiar home where several cars were parked outside. The house occupied a corner lot in one of the older neighborhoods in town. This house was built before the rest of the surrounding homes were developed, giving it a larger lot than the rest of the homes. Well-worn base paths betrayed how the extra land had been used over the years.

This was the home of my grandmother. Laughter floated out the back door of her home and down the steps to greet me. I could hear the voices of children inside. They shrieked with delight as a master storyteller thrilled them with tonight's tall tale. It was Monday night, and Roxy was entertaining guests.

Roxy's wispy grey hair was styled straight from the fifties. Her heart was young, but her body was nearing seventy-two, complete with wrinkles bearing evidence of many difficult years. Sometimes wrinkles are the scars of a difficult life. These were more like badges of perseverance.

Roxy had a spark—a gleam in her eye that invited you into her world. She was constantly on the go. She volunteered at church, The Salvation Army, and even sold programs at the racetrack on the south side of town. Every May, she organized a seniors' trip to the Indy 500. Her passions were driving and helping other people.

Nobody on earth could drive like Roxy. If women had been allowed to race in the Indy 500 when she was younger, she would have been able to prove it. Even though a four-lane highway had connected Bloomington to Indianapolis for several decades, she still preferred to take the twists and turns of Old State Road 37. The old highway snaked its way through beautiful countryside. Rolling hills, secluded valleys, and old farm country lined its two paved lanes. It cut through the Hoosier National Forest and met up with the new highway just south of the town of Martinsville.

When I was sixteen, I raced her from north Bloomington to Martinsville. I took the new road and she took the old. She beat me by ten minutes. I never told my parents because I was afraid they wouldn't let me see her again. But my grandmother meant the world to me. And boy, could she drive. Even though the old highway wound mercilessly in certain parts, she would speed through it laughing out loud all the way. Many of my older relatives believed that in her twenties, she could have won the Indy 500. I think she could win today!

Most people were terrified to ride with her. They would white-knuckle the dashboard or clutch their seatbelts and pray. However, if you could get past the fear, it was an inspiring thing to watch. She would laugh and hum old church hymns. The average person couldn't handle their grandma driving eighty mph in a forty mph zone, humming *Amazing Grace,* and laughing at memories she recalled to only herself.

I thought it was exhilarating. At nearly seventy-two, she was still living. A lot of people reach that age and haven't even started.

Roxy peered out behind thick, black, horn-rim glasses with the neck chain attached. She wore a blue flower print dress with a white lace collar. She stood only five feet, four inches, but she had a presence about her that made her seem much bigger. She was a Formula One driver masquerading as a Norman Rockwell painting.

Every Monday night Klondike, Darryl and I would go to Roxy's house for dinner. Sometimes Klondike would come with his wife and kids. The kids loved Roxy. They would circle around the kitchen table while she prepared the meal. Moving from pot to pan, oven to refrigerator, she spun tales of her childhood or recited children's classics from memory to the delight of the five little girls. It was their laughter that I heard as I came in without a knock. Roxy gave me a hug and motioned me to join the adults in the living room. All the while, she continued with her story.

The adults never had to be called to dinner. We knew it was ready when we heard shouts of glee from Klondike's daughters. Roxy, being the master entertainer, always came to the climax of the story just as the food was ready to serve. As the adults moved into the dining room, the girls trailed Roxy in from the kitchen as she gently led them to supper with the happy ending.

"The end," said Roxy. "Now, which one of you heathen boys is going to say the blessing?"

Abby, Klondike's six-year-old, jumped at the chance. "Dear God, thank you for this food and for Mommy and Daddy. Thank you for Miss Roxy and for her food and stories. Please let Mommy have another girl because boys are messy."

Klondike had taken a drink before the prayer, and he nearly choked on his iced tea. Bonnie had apparently let it slip to the girls, but still hadn't told her husband.

Abby continued, "I forgive you for taking my pet turtle Willard, but you had better be feeding him up in heaven." She started to say amen, but another request came to mind, "Oh wait, one more thing God. Please let Daddy and his friends buy the baseball team because they have cotton candy at baseball games. Amen."

It takes a child to remind us of the simple pleasures of going to the ballpark. While the entire town had visions of professional baseball, a rejuvenated economy, and national recognition, Abby saw an opportunity to have cotton candy more than once a year at the county fair.

"That was a good prayer, Abby," Roxy said. "So you boys are going to try to bring baseball to Bloomington. It's about time. Oh, I remember listening to Dodger games on the radio when Andy's grandfather was alive. It seems like they were playing the Yankees in the World Series every year."

"Do you think we're crazy?" Klondike asked.

"No, honey, I think you're crazy not to try. For most of my life, I've lived with one regret, that I never drove in a race. I never competed on the track. You see, I always admired Jackie Robinson for breaking through the color barrier and playing baseball. I always chased the little dreams. Some panned out and some didn't. But I never chased the big dream, the one I hid deep down inside. I wanted to drive in a race."

"Grandma, you still can," I interrupted. "You can still drive better and faster than anyone I know."

"Andy, no one is going to let an old woman in a race car today," she replied. "Too many people are afraid of being sued. Besides, it's not my dreams we're talking about. You boys have a dream. Remember when you were twelve?"

"Yes." Darryl and I looked at each other.

She looked at Jessica, Klondike's oldest daughter. "Honey, when those boys were your age, they used to play baseball in that side yard from sun up to sun down. One night they were playing catch just as the sun went down and they saw a shooting star. Have you ever seen a shooting star?"

Jessica's eyes widened and she shook her head. Roxy continued, "Well, when you see a shooting star, you're supposed to make a wish."

"What did you wish for?" Abby shouted.

"He wished for a baseball team in Bloomington. He and Darryl came running into this very kitchen, huffing and puffing, barely making sense. Darryl was convinced that Bloomington was going to get a baseball team. Andy had a little too much of his grandfather, the worrier, in him. He was excited but a little too skeptical."

"If he wished on the shooting star, what does he have to worry about?" Abby questioned. To her, it was that cut and dried. You make the wish and it comes true.

The years don't rob us of our youth as much as they rob us of wonder. Wonder lets us believe in the power of shooting stars. Roxy had just as much wonder in her heart as Abby. I realized then that there was something different about her that I hadn't noticed before. Like most of her family and friends, I was probably drawn to it without fully understanding why. Her life story would make a good book someday.

Later that night, after everyone else had gone home, Roxy looked at me sharply. "What's wrong?"

"What do you mean?"

"Don't try to fool me. I know when something's wrong with you."

"I'm a little scared."

"Scared of what?"

"Scared of losing the team to Roland Green. Scared of letting down the whole city."

"But it's not just your dream. They all own a piece of this dream. Nobody is going to point the finger at you if it doesn't work out."

"I know, but I got it started. I wrote the article."

"Do you remember your first day at work for the newspaper?"

"Yes."

"You came over that night all worried about the sports column you wrote. You kept telling me it was crap."

"And you kept telling me not to say 'crap.'"

"The point is you were so scared of failure that you were paralyzed. So the next article was crap." She paused. "Sorry, honey, that second article was awful."

She was right. "I knew you didn't like it," I said. "All these years and you've been holding out on me."

"Well, you're family. I didn't want to hurt your feelings." She grabbed my hands and looked me in the eyes. "But don't you remember the letters you got that first week? People really liked that first article."

"But not the second one?"

"Focus, child. Of course nobody liked the second one. It was crap."

"Grandma! I'm going to wash your mouth out with soap."

"You'd have to take my dentures out first. The point is you worried yourself over nothing. All these years later you've won awards and written some pretty good columns. It turned out OK, and so will this baseball thing. You worry too much, Andy. You always have. Do you remember that day you boys saw the shooting star?"

"Yes."

"You made that wish when you were twelve. Now it's coming true."

"Might be coming true," I said.

"You lack faith, child," she said. "What you need is faith that it's worth trying, not faith that it will happen. The consequences of failure are insignificant compared to the regret of not trying."

"But, I . . ."

She cut me off. "I pray for you, child. I pray for you every night. I pray that you'll stop worrying and have faith. I pray that you will not let the possible outcomes get in the way of doing things that are worth doing. And mostly, I pray that you'll stop wearing a sombrero when you're driving on South Walnut Street. I saw you the other day."

I thanked her for dinner and said goodbye. As I walked towards my car, I paused and then walked out into the yard to the very spot where I saw the shooting star. I stared at the sky for a few minutes, shook my head and whispered, "I don't know."

TEN

Keep Your Lawn Off My Body

(Money Raised: $27,543,983.35)

"The secret of managing is to keep the guys who hate you away from the guys who are undecided."

~ *Casey Stengel*

KATE AND PETE DECIDED TO have another shareholders' meeting at the convention center the week following the Council's approval of the new trolleys. The plan was to give shareholders an idea of how far we had come and what steps we were taking to get to our goal. The meeting also offered the opportunity to recruit new investors.

When Darryl and I arrived at the convention center, there was, of course, a protest happening. This one seemed unusually spirited given the recent amount of positive press we had received lately. From where we parked, there appeared to be two sides yelling and pointing at each other. The shareholders were forced to walk in between them to get to the front doors.

As we approached, we were able to read the signs. One read: "ABORTION IS MURDER!" On the opposite side, a sign read: "MY BODY, MY CHOICE!" We looked at each other. I looked back at the signs. Darryl looked up at the sky.

In the "What's Going On" section of that morning's newspaper, *Bloomington Daily News* intern, admitted pot smoker, and not-so-outstanding citizen Dusty Freeman had written that an abortion debate was being held that very night at the convention center. It was, in fact, being held at the IU Auditorium. Dusty covers Frisbee Golf tournaments now.

As we made our way through the gauntlet of protesters, I saw the most curious slogan on one of the pro-choice signs. It read: "KEEP YOUR LAWN OFF MY BODY." I paused. I turned my head to the side, not unlike a puppy that can't fathom what "sit" means. *Keep your lawn off my body*. I said it out loud: "Keep your lawn off my body."

"What did you say?" Darryl asked.

"That sign says, 'Keep your lawn off my body.'" I pointed towards the protesting anomaly. "What does that mean?"

"I have no idea," he answered.

"Keep your lawn off my body," I said it again. I kept saying it. There's some weird quirk in human nature that makes some people repeat things out loud when they don't understand them. I possess the quirk gene. I'm quirked.

Then I glanced back at the pro-life protesters. Had they been throwing sod at their opponents? That type of provocation would surely elicit a harsh response from the pro-choice crowd. Maybe they would start ripping out the shrubs that lined the parking lot and begin throwing them at the pro-life people. But a closer look at the pro-life side revealed clean hands. They hadn't been throwing sod. But who was putting *their* lawn on *her* body?

"Do you think we should—"

Darryl cut me off mid-sentence. "No, I don't think that's such a good idea."

At almost the same moment, I realized she had put an "n" where she meant to put an "s." I decided to go inside. It was time to talk about baseball.

Pete started the meeting off with a short statement and then turned the program over to Kate. She followed with a brief summary of our progress, announcing that as of the meeting, we had raised over $27 million. She then outlined our strategy to attract new investors. Finally, she opened up the meeting for questions. Most of the questions were pretty straightforward, and the meeting was about to wind up when The Wolf arrived.

The Wolf showed up at the meeting, wearing his best suit and carrying an alligator brief case. I made a mental note to report him to the remaining DWARVES. His two associate attorneys accompanied him, as well as his personal assistant and his legal secretaries. The Wolf liked to employ at least two secretaries between the ages of eighteen and twenty-two. His secretaries always looked like runway models and, of course, the rumors circulated around town as to what type of "legal" work they actually did.

When Kate noticed Plaything One and Plaything Two coming down the aisle, she cleared her throat. I glanced at her and she rolled her eyes. The entourage sat down and The Wolf went straight to the open microphone.

We couldn't keep him from buying shares, but we could keep him from holding any real power. Every time he tried to nominate himself for anything, we would vote him down. On this occasion, The Wolf planned to use the open question-and-answer time as a platform to trash Kate as general manager and me as media relations director.

"Fellow investors, this management team is ill suited to accomplish our goal of buying the Los Angeles Dodgers. We have barely raised ten percent of the total amount we are going to need to purchase the team. How could we possibly pin our hopes on a cosmetics saleswoman, a lucky inventor, the guy who runs the worst hotel in town, and the worst sports reporter in Indiana?" He paused as if waiting for applause or support. No one made a sound.

Darryl and Jesse were running the soundboard. I quietly made my way to the back of the room and grabbed a wireless microphone and a headset from Darryl. Just before I ducked behind the curtains, I motioned back to Darryl to cut The Wolf's microphone.

"Ladies and gentlemen, let's give a big round of applause to Mr. Wolf. You know, you've got to admire the persistence of a man who failed the bar exam seven times, but kept on taking it."

The Wolf was fuming and the rest of the crowd was looking around, trying to figure out where the voice was coming from. The Wolf tried to keep talking and motioned to Darryl to do something.

"And let's not forget his lovely assistants, Candy and Yvette. Stand up, ladies." They did, of course. "Folks, you can see more of Plaything One and Plaything Two in the September *Playboy* exposé 'Girls of the Legal Profession'! And finally, folks, I would be remiss if I didn't mention The Wolf's new business venture, Monarch Fitness, a place where steroids and creatine are more plentiful than middle-aged body builders trying to hook up with co-eds. But don't let the performance-enhancing drugs scare you away. Sure your testicles will shrivel to the size and color of raisins . . ." Five hundred people turned towards The Wolf. "But won't it be worth it to look like Arnold Schwarzenegger?"

Darryl immediately switched power to The Wolf's microphone, just in time for him to utter a stream of obscenities. Darryl could barely keep a straight face while explaining to his boss that he didn't know how someone had hijacked the audio feed. Meanwhile, I was still hiding behind the curtains and laughing so hard that tears ran down my face.

Once The Wolf composed himself, he walked back to the row where his entourage was sitting and motioned for them to leave. He waited in the aisle as they filed out. As Plaything One and Plaything Two stepped into the aisle, Plaything Two asked, "Are we really going to be in *Playboy*?"

The Wolf rolled his eyes, muttered a curse under his breath and pointed towards the back of the room. She got the hint and didn't ask any more questions. A chorus of giggles trailed The Wolf as he followed the entourage out of the main room, down the escalator, and out into the summer evening.

The laughter caused by The Wolf incident signaled the end of the meeting. I caught up with Kate and asked her how she liked my performance.

"That was you?" she asked.

"Of course. I couldn't stand by and let him talk about you that way. I was defending your honor."

"Well, thanks," she replied. "I guess I owe you one."

"How about going to Janko's?"

"Nope, not high enough on the chivalry meter."

"Hmm. You're tough. How about a baseball game? You don't even have to consider it a date. We can go with Pete and Darryl and a whole bunch of Trolley Dodgers, Inc., investors. Consider it a business trip."

"OK, I'll go to a game with you. You do mean the Indians, right?"

"Absolutely."

By the Indians, she was referring to the Indianapolis Indians. We usually went to Indy about twice a month to catch a game at Victory Field. The Indians were the Triple-A affiliate of the Cincinnati Reds. Indianapolis has a rich baseball tradition, dating back over one hundred years. Stars like Randy Johnson, Andres Gallaraga, Moises Alou, Pokey Reese and Aaron Boone played in Indianapolis. I figured a baseball game was the best way for Kate to observe me in my natural habitat.

"All right, just let me know what night. Mondays are bad for me. We do Mary Kay training on Monday nights."

"Fine, I'll check with the rest of the Freddys and let you know."

I left her and the rest of the management team to clean up. I had to write a quick story about the meeting for the next day's paper. The abortion/anti-abortion crowd had long since left. I noticed some of the signs from the protest were sticking out of the convention center's dumpster. I couldn't resist. The third sign I pulled out was the one I was looking for—Keep Your Lawn Off My Body. I thought it would look good in my office window.

ELEVEN

Pizza Dragons

(Money Raised: $34,685,493.35)

"That's why I don't talk. Because I talk too much."
~ *Joquin Andujar*

WE MADE PLANS TO GO TO the Indians game on the Friday after the shareholders' meeting. Klondike and Bonnie would meet us there. Kate planned to meet me at my apartment where Darryl would pick us up.

When I got home from work, I didn't have much time to get myself, or my apartment, ready for her visit. I looked at my watch—sixty-five minutes until Kate arrived. I raced from the car to my apartment door. Flinging the door open I let out a gasp. "OK, what sort of miscreants invaded my home?" I vowed to track them down later and soil their mothers' drapes.

A pile of clothes formed a tangled mass on my couch. They were clean clothes, just unfolded. A seldom-used exercise bike had a towel draped over it. Stacks of dishes lounged about the countertops. There was a dish party in the kitchen, and the clean dishes hadn't been invited. Evil green eyes peered out of a Pizza Express box. A pizza dragon would have to be slain.

I opened the dishwasher to find it surprisingly empty. Ah, much room to hide the dozens of glasses, plastic Pizza

Express cups, and cereal bowls. I quickly started rinsing things and shoving them into the dishwasher. Weeks of untidiness revealed some moldy cup bottoms. One glass contained a lump of milk.

After I filled every molecule of empty space in the dishwasher, I wiped down the counters. Then I elbowed the pizza box so it would fall on the floor. I refused to grab it, remembering the eyes. It landed flat on the diamond-patterned tile and a small cloud of crumbs escaped from the slightly open side. The dragon inside must breathe crumbs. I gently moved the box towards the front door with my foot. There it would stay until I could get the rest of the trash together.

The trash! How much time left? I had forty-seven minutes. I quickly grabbed the overloaded trash bags (four) that were piled in my utility closet. I carried them to the door, set them down, opened the door and kicked the pizza box onto the sidewalk. The dragon remained inside. I turned around to pick up the trash bags (now there were five—they're like rabbits) and noticed that a trail of some unidentified liquid had followed me from the closet to the front door. The toxic juice was emitting a rather malevolent odor.

The trip to the dumpster was slow going. I would kick the pizza box ahead of me and then watch for the dragon. When I felt comfortable that he would not appear, I would drag the trash bags to his new resting place and kick the box again. The last kick caused the box top to fly open. I dove behind the trash bags and covered my head in fear. When I was able to muster enough courage, I looked at the box with my head sort of turned away. Staring at me from the box were two shriveled jalapeños and a gnarled breadstick. Whew, that was a close one.

I quickly flung the trash into the dumpster and ran back to the apartment. Thirty-nine minutes. The congealed state of the clothes pile made it easy to grab and throw in a pile onto my closet floor. I wondered what she'd think if she could see my closet. Men and women have different views of walk-in closets. Women see a functional space for organizing one's wardrobe. Men see a dumping ground for the mess we don't want women to see. Celebrate our differences. You'll live longer.

Anyway, I was running out of time. A quick look at the bed revealed another pile of clothes and a mattress cover that was a third of the way off the mattress. No big deal, I thought. I'll just keep the bedroom door shut. I began to quickly take off my clothes while heading toward the shower. Walking and undressing should not be done when your mind is going in a thousand directions. As I tried to pull off my underwear, I tripped and fell face first onto the bathroom floor. When was the last time somebody mopped this place? I unstuck myself from the floor, and jumped into the shower.

By the time the shower was over, the bathroom mirror was steamed. I was afraid to look at the clock. Twenty-four minutes. No sweat, I thought. After some mandatory guy-grooming I ran back to the closet to pick out something to wear. Where were my clothes? I looked down. Then I looked back at the remaining clothes on the hangers. Then I looked back down. Looking up from the floor were the in-style, much wrinkled clothes. Peering down from the hanger were the older and don't-fit-so-well-anymore clothes.

The older and don't-fit-so-well-anymore clothes were ready to serve. The hip clothes needed maintenance. I didn't have time for maintenance. Only eleven minutes left. I compromised. I took a pair of shorts from the floor pile and an Indians golf shirt from the older clothes. We were just going to a baseball game.

I pushed the edge of the pile of clean clothes back into the closet so I could shut the door. Then it was off to the bathroom for more guy-grooming. I emerged from the bathroom and set about tidying up the living room. A highly efficient regimen of speed-dusting, speed-sweeping, and throwing things in closets and drawers made the place presentable.

Unfortunately it was during the exact moment the doorbell rang that I remembered the bathroom. The bathroom! The last sixty-five minutes of cleaning had been all for naught. One look at that bathroom and she would never want to see me again. As I opened the door, I wondered, how large *is* the female bladder? What are the odds she wouldn't have to use the bathroom before we left?

Kate looked, well, very un-Kate. Her usual Mary Kay suit had been replaced by denim shorts and a BoDeans T-shirt. My heart leapt; she liked the BoDeans! It sank immediately when she said, "Hey, how are you doing? Can I use your bathroom?"

Sure, I thought, let's get your nausea out of the way first. It will keep you from ordering any junk food at the game. "Go ahead; it's the first door on your left. It's a little messy. I apologize."

As she shut the door, I looked for a steak knife to impale myself upon. No luck; they were all crammed in the dishwasher. I heard coughing coming from the bathroom. I was sure she was launching her lunch. Isn't it funny how we get so nervous about what other people are thinking when we want them to like us? I was convinced that Kate was retching in my unkempt bathroom.

When she emerged, I tried to immediately get her mind off the filth she had just endured. "So, has it sunk in that you're the general manager of a baseball team?"

"Yes, but maybe I'm aiming too low."

"Maybe you're aiming too high."

"From the looks of your bathroom, I'd say *you're* not aiming at anything."

"Sorry, I meant to clean the place before you got here."

"Next time I'll give you a week's notice."

"Why a week?"

"There are bacteria in there picketing for better working conditions."

"I know, they're never satisfied. Last week it was for longer breaks and holiday pay."

That comment made her laugh. It was that unguarded laugh she had revealed at lunch. I liked that laugh. She plopped onto the couch.

"Is there a game on TV?" she asked.

I grabbed the remote and sat down next to her. "The Cubs are on WGN. They're playing the Padres. The Braves are playing the Marlins on TBS. We still have a few minutes before Darryl gets here, so we can watch an inning or two."

"Cubbies," she said. "Let's watch the Cubbies."

As I flipped on the TV, Harry Carray was going on about Tony Gwynn. "Stoney, that Tony Gwynn would look good in a Cubs uniform. And I'm sure Marge and Larry Cohen from Shaumberg, who are watching today, would love to see that too. Coming up to bat for the Cubs is Sammy Sosa. That's 'Asos' spelled backwards."

We both laughed. Harry Carray was every bit as entertaining as the game on the field. Given the history of the Cubs, more often than not he was way more entertaining than the game on the field.

"You're more into baseball than the average—"

"Than the average girl?" she cut me off.

"Well, that's not exactly where I was headed. OK, that's exactly where I was headed," I stammered. I'm sure my face was crimson by now.

"It's OK. I'll let it slide this time."

"That's so kind of you."

"I guess I'm into it because of heredity."

"Oh, did your dad play professionally or something?"

"Why did you assume it was my dad and not my mom?"

Now I was really squirming.

She giggled. "I just love to watch you squirm. Actually it was my great-grandmother."

"Your great-grandmother played professional baseball?"

"No, she is the most famous baseball fan of all time."

"I've never heard of her."

"But you sing about her every time you go to a game."

"Huh?"

"Pay attention; Harry is about to sing her song."

At this point I was completely stumped. She grabbed the remote, which set off the usual guy reaction to a woman having control of the remote: uncontrolled twitching. My twitching was combined with the puppy-dog head tilt as I tried to figure out what Harry Carray had to do with Kate's grandmother. Kate sang along with Harry and the rest of the Wrigley Field faithful as he led them in "Take Me Out to the Ballgame." When he was done, she turned the volume completely down and said, "Now, do you want to hear the rest of the song?"

"What rest of the song? That's all there is to it."

"And you call yourself a baseball fan? All you ever hear is the chorus. There are verses to that song. I'll sing them for you."

Then Kate sang "Take Me Out to the Ball Game" in its entirety:

Katie Casey was baseball mad,
Had the fever and had it bad;
Just to root for the hometown crew,
Ev'ry sou Katie blew.
On a Saturday her young beau
Called to see if she'd like to go,
To see a show, but Miss Kate said "No,
I'll tell you what you can do":

"Wait a minute, hold on," I interrupted. "What's a sou?"

"It's a nickel," she answered.

"Just to root for the home town crew, every *nickel* Katie blew," I repeated. "OK, now I get it."

"May I continue?"

"Please do."

Take me out to the ball game,
Take me out to the crowd.
Buy me some peanuts and Cracker Jack,

I don't care if I ever get back,
Let me root, root, root for the home team,
If they don't win it's a shame.
For it's one, two, three strikes you're out,
At the old ball game.

Katie Casey saw all the games,
Knew all the players by their first names;
Told the umpire he was wrong,
All along, good and strong.
When the score was just two to two,
Katie Casey knew what to do,
Just to cheer up the boys she knew,
She made them sing this song:

Take me out to the ball game,
Take me out to the crowd.
Buy me some peanuts and Cracker Jack,
I don't care if I ever get back,
Let me root, root, root for the home team,
If they don't win it's a shame.
For it's one, two, three strikes you're out,
At the old ball game.

"Most people believed the woman in the song was just made up. Katie Casey was a real person. The guy who wrote the words, Jack Norworth, was courting my great-grandmother. Legend has it he had the inspiration while riding a train that passed right by the Polo Grounds."

"Where the Giants used to play—"

She cut me off, "And the Yankees before they moved to Yankee Stadium." I don't know what impressed me most; that "Take Me Out to the Ballgame" was written about her great-grandmother or that she knew the Yankees and Giants shared the Polo Grounds. From that point on, whenever she took the remote, I didn't twitch. I think that might be the sign of true love—when a person doesn't make you twitch.

Just then we heard Darryl honking his horn.

TWELVE

Tribe Fries

(Money Raised: $34,686,493.35)

(Klondike made a deposit on the way to the game.)

"Guys ask me, don't I get burned out? How can you get burned out doing something you love? I ask you, have you ever got tired of kissing a pretty girl?"

~ *Tommy Lasorda*

WE MET KLONDIKE AND PETE outside the ticket windows at Victory Field. Bonnie and the girls had decided to stay home. The Indians were playing Oklahoma City that night, and most of the tickets had been sold. We didn't know it ahead of time, but it was Win a Car Night. Every year the Indians have a night where fans can win a used car. Local dealers provide ten used cars for the giveaway. Some are really nice, and others are total clunkers. I was hoping to upgrade the Scarlet Cricket.

We were lucky enough to find five seats together down the third base line. The seats gave us a great view of the Indianapolis skyline and the RCA Dome, home of the Indianapolis Colts. Our seats were located in the second row, just across the wall from where the bullpen catcher warmed up the pitchers. We took our seats and settled in for the game.

"Tell her the Bun Fairy story," Darryl said.

"What's the Bun Fairy story?" she asked.

"You can help me tell it, in case I forget something. Darryl and I went to Detroit a few years ago. It was early May, so the weather in Detroit was pretty lousy. We were in line at the concession stand for what seemed an eternity. When we finally got to the front, Darryl ordered a hot dog and a hot chocolate."

Darryl continued, "The guy behind the counter grabbed a hot dog with some tongs and opened a drawer to get the bun. Apparently, the bun drawer was empty. He looked around for a few minutes obviously baffled. The idea that the bun supply could be depleted had never entered his mind. Finally, he asked for help, and a co-worker told him where the buns were stored."

"So then, I made Darryl a bet," I added. "I bet him that the guy would come back with only one bun."

"I thought, surely he's not that dumb," Darryl said.

"But he overestimated the hot dog vendor," I said. "The man returned bearing a single bun."

"I started laughing as he put the hot dog in the bun. As soon as I paid, Andy told me to watch him do it again."

"I ordered the exact same thing, and yes, the concession guy opened the drawer where the buns are kept and was again surprised to see *no* buns." Turning directly to Kate, I added, "At this point we surmised that Detroit must have a Bun Fairy. It is the Bun Fairy's job to go from one concession stand to another and distribute hot dog buns. The fact that this employee couldn't possibly conceive of the idea that he could reload the bun drawer himself convinced me that Detroit concession stand workers believe wholeheartedly in the Bun Fairy. And when the Bun Fairy fails to replenish the buns, chaos and confusion seize hold of the ballpark staff, filling them with dread."

"The Bun Fairy," she said. "I like that. Maybe at Gomez Park we could incorporate the Bun Fairy." Klondike and Pete seemed to like the idea.

During the fifth inning, the Indians pitcher started to get hit pretty hard. They began warming up a reliever just in front of us. Since we were close to the aisle, we witnessed a comical exchange between a couple of drunken rednecks and the bullpen catcher. The rednecks were demanding that the catcher give their son a baseball. The kid was in no way deserving of a ball, inasmuch as he had pushed another child down the steps during the second inning when a foul ball was hit our way. The more they yelled at the catcher, the more puzzled his face looked. The more he didn't respond, the more riled up they became. Eventually, the ushers had to escort them out of the stadium. During the whole exchange, I kept laughing harder and harder.

"How could you think that rude display was funny?" Kate asked.

"Because they don't know a thing about baseball, and he doesn't know a thing about English."

"What?"

"If those hillbillies had a clue about the Indians roster, they would know that the catcher is Roberto Pena. Pena arrived here yesterday as part of a three-way trade between the Reds, Brewers, and Detroit. Pena doesn't speak a word of English. They could have been shouting lines from *Seinfeld* and he wouldn't have known the difference."

"So, you think you know your baseball trivia, do you?" she asked.

"Oh, no, here we go," Klondike cautioned.

"Are you challenging me to a baseball trivia contest?" I asked.

"Not just you," she answered. "I'll take on all four of you."

"Wager time. Who's in?" Pete asked.

"Let's make this interesting. Instead of playing for money, let's play for humiliation," Darryl said. "The losers have to do something embarrassing for them. For example, if I lose, I'll come to work in a kilt."

"No way," I said. "You work on the radio. If you lose, you have to teach your first class of the semester in a kilt."

"Deal. What about you?" he asked.

"If I lose, I'll deliver flowers to The Wolf."

"I'm out," Klondike said. "I always lose these things."

"Me too," Pete added. "Klondike and I will be the judges."

"OK, the rules are we ask one question of one contestant. As soon as you miss two questions in a row, you're out," Kate said.

"Wait a minute, what about you?" I asked.

"What about me?"

"What is your embarrassing thing going to be?"

"Well if I *lose*, which I won't, then we can think of something."

"No, no, no," Darryl said. "Everybody knows the stakes up front."

"I say if you lose, you have to ride on the Trolley Dodgers float during the Fourth of July parade in a blue prom dress and a crown on your head."

"You're on," she answered confidently.

And thus began a great trivia question contest. Many challenging questions were fired back and forth. I put Darryl out with the question of who went the longest period of times between wins as a pitcher: Babe Ruth. Kate matched me question for question until the sixth inning when we paused for Macho Mike Sullivan to lead the crowd in a chorus of the Village People's "YMCA." Mike is a largish fellow who has worked for the Indians for as long as I can remember. Every home game, he gets up on the third base dugout and dances to "YMCA." Baseball is ruled by tradition.

During Mike's performance, the winning question hit me. "The Yankees have won the most championships in Major League Baseball," I said. "Next to the Yankees, what franchise—in the minor leagues—has won the most championships?"

"Oh, that's brutal," Klondike said.

I gave her an entire inning to guess and even let her consult with Pete, Darryl, and Klondike. "The Durham Bulls, Louisville, no Columbus," they shouted.

I laughed and shook my head. "It's the Indians."

"What? These Indians?" Kate said.

"Fourteen championships have been won by *these* Indians."

Kate glared at me. "That's a pretty cheesy question for me to have to wear a prom dress. I want a ruling from the judges."

"No, I have to go with Andy," Pete said. "He stumped all of us with that one."

And so I successfully forced Darryl and Kate to have to wear dresses. I hoped that she wouldn't hold the grudge too long. Darryl I wasn't worried about. He probably liked the idea of freaking out a class of freshmen.

To make the night even more wonderful, I was the winner of the eighth inning Win a Car drawing. My upgrade from the Scarlet Cricket: a yellow AMC Pacer.

Aaron Baker won the game for the Indians, hitting a home run in the bottom of the ninth. We said goodbye to Pete and Klondike and headed to the office to pick up the keys to my newly-acquired Pacer. We had planned to split up so I could drive the car home but it wouldn't start. I had to have it towed back to Bloomington. Darryl decided to drop Kate off at her house first, mostly because both he and I were curious about where she lived. Of course, it was way too dark to really get a feel for the size of it, but I could tell it was huge. We pulled into her driveway, and I walked her to her door.

"You're not still mad at me about the trivia contest, are you?"

She slid her hand through my arm. "Of course not. It's hard to stay mad at you, Andy Bennett."

"So, how long has it been since you had a really good kiss goodnight?"

"About ten years. That's how I fell in love with my ex-husband."

"Have you ever wondered what it would be like to kiss a sports reporter in the moonlight, with nobody watching?"

"Darryl's watching."

"Who's Darryl?"

I kissed her.

"I don't remember."

She kissed me.

"Me, either."

We kissed each other.

"You realize if we do buy the team, I'll be your boss," she said. "We won't be able to do this in public."

"Fire me."

"Good idea."

We kissed again. This kiss lasted much longer, after which she leaned against her front door with her eyes closed. She smiled, opened her eyes and said goodnight. I turned back to the street and said, "It's missing." I paused and looked around. "I'm supposed to ride off on a horse."

She was still laughing as I said goodnight and headed for the car. Darryl didn't say anything for a whole thirty seconds. "You know she'll be your boss if we buy the team."

"We've got it all worked out."

"How?"

"She's going to fire me."

"Huh. Good plan."

Darryl pulled out of her driveway and took me home.

THIRTEEN

Wiffle Ball

(Money Raised: $49,394,223.35)

"In Brooklyn, it was as though you were in your own little bubble. You were all part of one big, but very close family, and the Dodgers were the main topic of everybody's conversations and you could sense the affection people had for you. I don't know that such a thing exists anymore."
~ *Don Drysdale*

OVER THE NEXT FEW WEEKS, money and pledges started to pour in. Kate and Pete hit the road again to meet with potential investors. Darryl hit the airwaves every day and I sent media kits all over the country. By the first week of July, we were totally drained. One particular Thursday afternoon, we sat exhausted at Trolley Dodgers headquarters. It was more mental fatigue than physical. We needed to be energized. We needed a shot of adrenaline. We needed to play wiffle ball.

"Have you ever played wiffle ball?" I asked.

"Not since I was seven," Kate said.

Pete, Darryl, Klondike and I looked at each other in disbelief.

"Roxy's!" we said in unison.

"Do you have any clothes in your car you can change into?" I asked.

"No, why do I need—"

"You'll need to run by your house and change," I cut her off. "Tennis shoes, shorts, and a T-shirt." I quickly wrote down the way to Roxy's house. "Do these directions make sense?"

"Yeah, I think I can find it. What are we doing?"

"Just be there in thirty minutes."

I called Roxy on the way.

When Kate arrived, we were already warming up. Some neighborhood kids had joined us for the game.

"I didn't think grownups still played wiffle ball."

"That's why we don't let any near this place," I said.

The kids laughed. Roxy's side yard was a magical place—a juvenile Garden of Eden. Everyone who stepped onto that field was twelve again. In the movie *Field of Dreams*, Ray Kinsella builds a baseball field that brings back dead ballplayers. Roxy's side yard brought back dead childhoods.

We played until the sun got tired and went home, making the ball hard to see. I can't recall how many games we played. We altered the teams every five innings or so. Kate played as well as any of the guys. She confessed she had played softball four years in high school. She seemed a little sad when she told us that she wished she could have played in college. It lasted only a moment, though, because that's the power of Roxy's side yard.

Roxy noticed Kate through the kitchen window and came out to introduce herself. She was making cookies and cakes and all sorts of goodies for a bake sale at her church. Otherwise she would have been outside watching us. However, in her usual hospitable manner, every few innings she came out with drinks or snacks or just to give us the score of the Cubs game.

By the time we finished, there were thirteen people playing. More kids from the neighborhood had joined at various points. We didn't have an even number of players per team, but since one of the boys was only five, it didn't matter. It also didn't matter who won or lost. We just played.

Some of the kids' parents had come down to watch as well as a couple who had been walking their dog. Roxy made sure they had plenty to drink. Every time we played, the parents of the neighborhood kids would thank us over and over again. And Roxy would always invite them back to play any time. When we were kids, the only thing that prevented a game at Roxy's was a storm, and it better be a thunderstorm, because we didn't mind playing in the rain. Every day we played, all summer long. Now the games at Roxy's were few and far between. The neighborhood kids had discovered PlayStations, GameBoys, and a host of other reasons not to go outside. They only seemed to play when we came around. Maybe that's why their parents were so grateful.

As the summer wore on, and the town became more wrapped up in buying the Dodgers, the neighborhood kids started to play more wiffle ball at Roxy's house. She even bought a small storage shed to hold bases, bats, and balls. By August, there was a game at Roxy's every day—just like when we were kids.

After we said goodbye to all the kids and their parents, Pete and Klondike left. Darryl, Kate and I sat on Roxy's back porch. With the porch lights out, you could see stars to the south. The porch was screened and held a porch swing, wicker chairs and a wicker love seat. Darryl sat in the love seat with his feet propped on the coffee table. I did the same, sitting in one of the wicker chairs. Kate lay on the porch swing. One leg stuck out over the armrest, and the other dropped on the ground below. Using that leg, she gently rocked herself. We probably stayed there for another two hours, sometimes talking, sometimes listening to the crickets and observing the occasional firefly. Through an open window we could hear Roxy moving about the kitchen and humming some Glenn Miller tune.

After a while, Roxy finished in the kitchen and joined us on the porch. She sat next to Darryl on the love seat. He leaned his head on her shoulder for a while. Roxy was everybody's grandma.

"So how close are you kids to buying that baseball team?"

"We still have a long way to go," I said. "As of yesterday we were still stuck around $50 million. Is that about right, Kate?"

"Yeah, it's pretty close to that," she answered.

"We still have a lot of money to raise and we're running out of time. Maybe this town really isn't big enough for the major leagues." I hesitated. "It still seems pretty crazy, doesn't it?"

"Oh, I don't know," Roxy said. "Sometimes a dream is too big *not* to go after. And this one seems pretty big. You're not getting cold feet, are you?"

I pondered her words for a while.

"Are you getting cold feet?" Kate sat up on the porch swing.

"No, no. Roxy already talked me out of quitting. I'm just . . ." I thought for a second. "I just don't know what it would do to this town if we failed. I don't know what it would do to me if it failed."

"Big dreams always bring the possibility of big failures," Kate said. "It's how life works!"

"I don't think this town will suffer," Darryl said. "We've gotten a lot of positive publicity from this. I think it will increase tourism no matter what. Besides, I've thought if we got close and failed, we might have a shot for a minor league franchise."

"I never thought of that," I said. "You're right. This might just position us for a Double A team."

Kate was emphatic. "Hold it right there. You guys have to be behind this thing one hundred percent. We're not playing for a minor league team down the road. We're playing for the Dodgers, *now*. Focus on what we're going to do *when* we win! Don't start thinking about what we're going to do if we fail. I would never allow any of my Mary Kay Sales Directors to talk like that. *We are going to buy the Dodgers*!"

"I like her," Roxy said. "You boys need to pay attention to her."

For quite a while I said nothing. The conversation turned to baking and road work on the bypass, but I was still digesting Roxy's words: Some dreams are too big not to pursue. I had never fully understood why so many people had jumped on board so fast. We had batted around the idea of a minor league team in Bloomington for years, and few people seemed to care. A minor league team in a town this size was much more realistic, much more doable. But this—this was huge. These were the same Dodgers that included Jackie Robinson, Tommy Lasorda, Pee Wee Reese, and Duke Snyder. Those Dodgers, in *Bloomington*? Yet, here was a college town filled with every type of competing interest group, united by a common goal. It seemed too big and too outrageous to get my arms around. Some dreams are too big not to pursue? OK, I thought, let's find out.

I was startled out of my deep thought by laughter. "Oh come on, it will open up a whole new world to you guys," I heard Kate pleading.

"I'll go if he goes," Darryl said.

"What are you Freddys talking about?"

"Where have you been for the last five minutes? We're talking about you, Darryl, and Klondike joining me at a huge Mary Kay event."

"Right."

"What's the matter?" Kate fired back. "Are you afraid of a few hundred women armed with cosmetics and good attitudes?"

"Do I have to put on make-up?"

"No, you idiot. I just want you to get a glimpse of my world."

"You should go," Darryl said.

"You're going with me!"

"No, I think I'll sit this one out," he replied.

"You're both going!" Roxy ordered. "You both have jobs and cars and college degrees but you still act like twelve-year-olds. It's settled. You're both going, and you're taking Klondike with you."

"Why does he have to go?" Darryl asked.

"To keep you two in line," she replied. "Lord knows, he's got a house full of girls so he should know how to behave in a room full of women."

Roxy got up laughing and went into the kitchen.

"Well, it looks like two weeks from this Monday you boys are going to learn all about Mary Kay." Kate laughed. "We can meet at the Trojan Horse at six. That will give us time to eat and get over to the convention center. The meeting starts at seven-thirty."

"How are you going to get Klondike to go?" I asked.

"That's easy," Darryl said. "Kate, are there free samples at these meetings?"

"Sometimes," she answered. "Why?"

"Five daughters," he said.

"And one on the way," I added.

FOURTEEN

Bagels, Bubble Gum, and Beer

(Money Raised: $89,000,003.35)

"You can observe a lot by watching."

~ *Yogi Berra*

THE FOURTH OF JULY IS a magical day in America. The full spectrum of political debate is washed away by a crimson and blue tide, with white foamy breakers. The question of whether to grill hamburgers or hot dogs is about the liveliest debate you'll find. Having never lived on either coast, I don't know how the rest of the country views the Fourth. But in Middle America, our slower pace slows a little more.

That is, of course, if you're not part of a parade. Fortunately for me, I was covering it and free from float responsibilities. Bloomington's annual parade was probably no different than most American small-town parades. Nearly the whole town turned out, and there was lots of pomp and circumstance from the local government.

Trolley Dodgers, Inc., had voted to put together a float to promote the team and invited the local Little League Dodgers to ride on the float and throw candy to the crowd. We were able to order gumballs with baseball seams and the team name printed in blue.

Because Kate had lost the trivia contest, she had to ride on the float in a Dodger-blue formal gown with a tiara on her head. She sat on a throne (a stadium seat from old Comiskey Park) that was resting in a large fielder's glove made out of tissue paper and chicken wire. The glove rested on a flat trailer covered in green Astroturf. On each corner was a large plastic baseball filled with gumballs. Three Little Leaguers were assigned per corner to throw gumballs at the crowd. Kate wore a white satin sash embellished with pink letters screaming "Trolley Dodgers"! The trailer was pulled by a bright blue tractor, loaned to us by a local farmer for the day.

The staging area for the parade was the convention center parking lot. I arrived a little late, so all of our people were already there. I wasn't going to ride the float, but I wanted to see them off and of course, tease Kate.

At the sign-in table, I was given a directory of the floats in the order they would be leaving. To save time they had abbreviated some of the participant names. Trolley Dodgers wasn't on the first page, so I flipped to the second page where four words were printed: Gay Librarians Dodge Bagels. Ominous music began to play in my head.

I assumed this meant our float was next to last, so I worked my way through the crowds of people who were hurrying the other way to find a good place to watch the parade. When I arrived, I saw we had been placed between the Volunteer Librarians of America (VLOA) and the Bagel Company. Ahead of the librarians were the Gay American Celtic Troubadours (GACT, for short). Just ahead of GACT was State Senator Cochrane on a float to honor Monroe County war veterans. Unfortunately for the senator, the librarians and the troubadours had been lobbying the senator for money, support and recognition for quite some time. Both groups seized upon his proximity in order to voice their agendas.

I must say that GACT had the most breathtaking float in the parade. It depicted the Emerald Isle and the United States, connected with a rainbow bridge with a pot of gold at the end. The "gold" was actually gold foil-covered chocolate coins that they would throw to the crowd. The troubadours were dressed in authentic Irish costumes, each with an American flag pin on his chest. Red, white and blue bunting bordered the float.

Despite being an openly heterosexual male, I didn't feel the least bit uneasy visiting the GACT float. You see, they always had the best pre-parade beer and were more than generous in sharing it with their neighbors. However, as I drank my beer, I could hear animosity brewing between the leader of GACT and the head volunteer librarian. Both were demanding time after the parade with the senator. His press secretary tried to position himself between the senator and the advancing citizens.

The news reporter in me took over and I began taking notes in between sips of beer. Chad Penny spoke for troubadours and Juanita Root represented the librarians. She kept telling Chad to "ssh!" Danny Banks, the senator's press secretary, kept insisting that the honorable senator wanted the afternoon off just like every other American. Inserting myself into the debate, I raised my glass and said, "Hear, hear!" To which the librarian told me to "ssh," and Chad ordered one of the troubadours to get me another beer. Before I could blink, a troubadour was handing me a fresh drink. I thanked him and continued to listen to the exchange.

"The Volunteer Librarians of America are a formidable voting block," Juanita said. "I suggest you take that into consideration. The last thing the senator needs in an election year is to incur the wrath of the VLOA."

"This isn't an election year," I pointed out.

Juanita told me to "ssh" again. Chad eyed my beer, and satisfied that it was almost full, returned to the conversation.

"We just want a hearing from Senator Cochrane about our petition to the National Endowment for the Arts," said Chad. "The NEA has ignored us as legitimate torch bearers of an ancient yet historically significant art form."

The press secretary, obviously frazzled by the barrage of special interest groups, appeared to be on the verge of a nervous breakdown. At that point, I decided to intervene on his behalf. I set my beer down, jumped up and put my arm around the press secretary.

"Relax. Take a deep breath," I said. "What you need is a few moments to yourself. I shouted to the troubadours, "Get this man a beer!" Instantly a beer was in my hand and I gently held it up to his mouth. "Here, drink this. It will calm your nerves." He took a sip, and then took the cup from my hand. "Now, lie down on the float for a second."

He sat down on the float, feet dangling off the edge. Then he leaned back, his head resting next to a black pot with gold coins inside. Above his head, the bright blue Indiana sky was cut in half by a rainbow made of fresh flowers. I motioned for the troubadours to gather around the press secretary. I told them to sing, and the sweet harmony of "O, Danny Boy" was carried along on the July breeze. The song managed to soothe the press secretary's nerves, while raising the ire of Mrs. Juanita Root. When the singing started, Juanita made straight for the defenseless senator. Just then, the floats began to move out, forcing Juanita to abandon her mission to bend the senator's ear and return to her float. When the song concluded, I filled my glass and grabbed another for Kate (a peace offering for the electric blue prom dress she was wearing).

The floats were starting to leave the parking lot, and as I walked away, I turned, held up my glass in salute, and shouted, "Godspeed, troubadours! Godspeed!"

Kate looked at the glass longingly for a fraction of a second and then shook her head.

"It's going to be hard enough to retain my dignity and composure under the present circumstances. Alcohol will only make it worse. I can't believe I lost that trivia contest."

"I thought you said you weren't mad about it," I reminded her.

"Well, it was a lot easier to be a good sport before I saw this dress!"

"You look gorg—"

She put her index finger on my lips and gave me the eye. The eye said, "If the word *gorgeous* comes out of your mouth, I'll rip out your tongue and scratch out your eyes."

Out of the corner of my eye I saw that the librarians were already moving forward. I took a step backward. "I'll see you after the parade."

Kate was not particularly excited about spending the next hour riding a float, sitting in a baseball glove surrounded by twelve-year-old boys, some of whom had recently discovered girls. The shortest of the boys had discovered Kate in particular, and followed her around like a puppy. A few of the boys discovered they could hit the kids on the bagel float with gumballs. The kids on the bagel float could also reach the Trolley Dodgers' float with bagels, so a really entertaining war was brewing.

I found Darryl and Klondike at the space where the radio station float had been. Klondike's daughters were riding on that float. Klondike had stopped entering a float to promote his hotel a few years back after an incident involving Shetland ponies, chili dogs and a man playing a bagpipe.

The convention center parking lot was cluttered with debris, tables, and the nearly lifeless bodies of people who had made too many trips to the troubadours' keg. Darryl, Klondike and I made our way to the Square and found a space that Bonnie had saved for us. Our spot was on the corner of Kirkwood and Walnut, towards the end of the parade route.

After about thirty minutes, we could see the first of the floats. Leading the way was the Bloomington North High School marching band. They played "Stars and Stripes Forever" to the delight of everyone. Nearly everyone had a small flag to wave and anyone not wearing red, white and blue stood out from the crowd.

A few memorable and not so memorable floats passed by, making way for The Wolf and his new business venture: Monarch Fitness Centers. Bodybuilders and fitness models waved American flags and posed for the crowd. Perched high above them was The Wolf—seated on a throne in all his self-important glory. The crowd marveled at the body builders and fitness models, and then they laughed at the little man perched on his throne.

Immediately following The Wolf was a rolling carnival midway, complete with a ring toss and a balloon popping game. At the back end, a man appeared to be guessing people's weight. The sign said it all: Future Karnies of America. I noticed that Darryl was as delightfully horrified as I was.

"Isn't Carnies spelled with a *c*?" I asked.

"Does it matter?"

"Well, you've got me there."

A few floats later, Klondike's daughters entertained the crowd by throwing candy and key chains from the radio float. Bonnie had a smile a mile wide; she and Klondike took at least a roll of pictures each. I caught Abby's eye and winked at her. She jumped up and down and waved to me.

After twenty more minutes, we could see the final group of floats making their way down Kirkwood Avenue for the grand finale. The trouble began, not unlike much that is peculiar in this world, with a couple of wayward Shriners. These two had been lurking about the GACT float for nearly two hours prior to the start of the parade. And I must say that they enjoyed the hospitality of the troubadours. So much so that by the time the parade started, they were legally drunk.

Through most of the parade, they seamlessly blended their drunkenness with the usual Shriner mini-car hijinks. Nothing they did raised suspicion from onlookers. That changed, however, when they passed by our location. For some strange reason, at that very moment they decided to play chicken.

At a breakneck speed of four mph, they charged at each other. Reckless abandon consumed their minds (probably contained in their funny hats) as they came closer and closer. Neither man flinched. Or turned. So they hit head on at a speed fast enough to knock the red fez off Shriner A into the lap of Shriner B. This started a round of gratuitous vomiting from Shriner B into the upside down fez in his lap. Now, the entertainment value of two men in their sixties playing chicken in mini-cars can only be eclipsed by a food fight between politicians, gay troubadours, and volunteer librarians. Which is, of course, exactly what happened next.

The Shriners caused a roadblock that forced the final five floats to pull alongside each other, filling the entire intersection of Kirkwood and Walnut. Closest to us was the Trolley Dodgers float. Next to it were the troubadours, followed by the senator, the librarians, and the Bagel Company pulled up on the far side.

The VLOA seemed extremely agitated and a bit irrational. It was later discovered that the ladies had, in fact, been drinking hard cider for the past three hours and were as drunk as the two Shriners waiting for a tow. This is not to say that the troubadours were any less sober, inasmuch as they had a keg with them on the float. I noticed that the senator's press secretary was still relaxing on the troubadours' float.

I'm embarrassed to say that our Little Leaguers fired the first volley. Some of the boys, in a last ditch attempt to show their physical prowess to Kate and thus win her heart, tried to throw gumballs as far as they could. As far as they could turned out to be as far as the librarians' float, except for one very large boy who hit the bagel float.

And so it began: The Great Bagel/Gumball War. The gumball that hit the bagel float struck a teenage boy in the back of the head. He wheeled around and started throwing bagels at no one in particular. Three of the gumballs that hit the VLOA float did, in fact, strike Mrs. Juanita Root, who had consumed a half quart of hard cider in an effort to console herself for not securing a private meeting with the senator. To the chagrin of librarians everywhere, volunteer and professional, her next act would prompt a judge to order her never to be caught within one hundred feet of the honorable and outstanding citizen, Senator Douglas Cochrane.

She let out a loud cry and shouted something about the wrath of Biblio, the pagan god of reference works. And with that she grabbed a wooden newspaper holder from the float display and threw it in the general direction of the troubadours. It sailed through the air, but the newspaper was still in it, causing considerable drag. The poor aerodynamics combined with the limited strength of the sixty-three-year-old arm of Juanita Root caused the projectile to fall short of its target. Instead of hitting the troubadours, the newspaper holder hit the senator in the back, knocking him to the ground.

Kate was frozen in horror as the scene degenerated into a war zone. I sensed she needed rescuing, or maybe it was the beer. I leapt off the curb, took two steps, and jumped onto the float. I was struck in the head repeatedly by bagels but I was undaunted! Speeding to my queen in the bright blue dress, I grabbed her arm. She turned away from the melee with a startled expression. Realizing she needed to get off the float immediately, Kate followed me to the back of the trailer.

I jumped off first and then helped her down as gently as possible. "Save yourself," I yelled melodramatically. "Run for the sidewalk." A bagel whizzed between our heads. "And keep your head down."

"What are you going to do?" she asked.

"There's one more soldier to save," I replied. I got Darryl's attention and he met me at the back of the float.

"The beer?" he asked.

"The beer," I replied.

We dodged bagels and gumballs to reach the troubadours' float. On the back of the float was a troubadour grasping the keg and covering his head. At first he feared us, but when we didn't hit him with anything, he released the keg. "Grab the cups and keep your head down," I ordered him. Darryl and I hoisted the keg and sprinted for the sidewalk. Only a third of the beer was left, so we were able to move it quickly.

Upon arriving at the sidewalk, I bowed before Kate, who slapped me on top of the head. "Stop that. I could really use something to drink. Do you have anything besides beer?"

I grabbed her a soda out of Klondike's cooler and hugged her.

"I'm so glad you're alive," I said. "I feared you would be killed, My Queen."

"You're lucky I'm so thirsty or I'd pour my drink over your head." Her lack of gratitude was stunning.

"What? No kiss for your rescuer?" I asked.

"No," she replied, but she was smiling.

I filled up everyone's cups because the troubadour was too traumatized to man the keg. And so we watched and drank beer as the police broke up the riot. On this, our most patriotic of holidays, with "America the Beautiful" playing in the background, children enjoyed a food fight while a normally mild-mannered librarian tried to pull the toupee off a drunken press secretary. I held my glass high, waved a small American flag, and took comfort knowing that bagels, bubblegum, and beer must have been on the list of reasons we fought the British for our independence.

It was the most shocking event in the century old tradition of the annual Fourth of July parade in Bloomington, Indiana, USA. An Indianapolis news cameraman captured most of it on tape, and we were once again on CNN. Luckily, he was shooting from the opposite side of the street, so Trolley Dodgers, Inc. avoided any bad publicity. The VLOA voted unanimously to dismiss Juanita Root. The troubadours were noticed by a national record label which gave them a lucrative recording contract. The owner of the Bagel Company, displaying a sense of humor about the whole thing, introduced the bagel with a gumball in the middle, which is still their biggest seller. Senator Cochrane had to find a new press secretary because Danny became the troubadours' agent.

As for me, I hurried out a story for the next day's paper, then picked up Kate at her house and drove to the Pointe on Lake Monroe. We had made plans earlier to join Darryl, Klondike and their families to watch fireworks.

We parked near a friend's condo and walked along a winding path leading to the lake. The way was partially lit by the moon, but I took Kate's hand so she wouldn't stumble. At the end of the path was a private boat dock. The moonlight reflected off the water, illuminating a small pontoon boat. We climbed aboard and I untied it from the dock.

"Where are the others?"

"They're watching from the marina," I answered.

"I thought you said we were watching the fireworks with Darryl, Klondike and their families."

"We are. They're just going to be on the shore, and we'll be on the water. Do you mind?"

"No, I guess not." She sounded confused.

I started the engine and we pulled away from the dock. We made our way around a small peninsula then steered toward the center of the reservoir. Lights from other boats welcomed us to the party. I stopped the engine, tossed the anchor, and turned on a small light. That was when Kate noticed the cooler.

"What's in that?"

I opened it. "Well, we have champagne, two glasses, and chocolate-covered strawberries."

"How long have you been planning this?"

"Weeks. Are you impressed, surprised, angry?"

"Delighted," she whispered and kissed me on the cheek.

Only moments after I poured the champagne, the fireworks began. I quickly turned off the light and slowly the other boats went dark. For the next half hour, we watched in silence as little white fireballs raced towards the moon. Somewhere along the way, each would erupt into a billion glowing particles—red, green, and purple. Golden arcs with blue-flame tips gave way to thunderous cannon blasts. Each glowing particle would slowly descend, reflecting off the water below. Some were extinguished by the ride down, while others kissed the water goodnight.

For whatever reason—champagne, strawberries, the rocking of the boat—we stopped paying attention to the fireworks. We did stop kissing long enough to see the last few seconds of the grand finale. When the fireworks faded and moonlight recaptured the sky, a lonely glowing particle drifted over our heads and sizzled as it landed in my champagne glass. Around the lake, lights slowly appeared, betraying the positions of the other boats. As I reached to turn on our light, Kate grabbed my hand.

"Don't," she said. "We haven't seen all the fireworks yet." She gently pushed me back into my seat. "Happy Fourth of July."

FIFTEEN

The Menace From the East

(Money Raised: $89,000,503.35)

"When they said Ebbets Field was too small, too dilapidated, I took it as a personal insult. I couldn't imagine a more beautiful place."

~ *Doris Kearns Goodwin*

I THOUGHT IT WOULD TAKE YEARS for me to find a more bizarre story than the Bagel/Gumball War. It took less than a day. When we embarked on this journey, we knew we would encounter a great deal of resistance. Beyond the protests in our own backyard, we knew the fans in Los Angeles would not take this lying down. We also expected some flak from baseball purists. Unfortunately, we never looked for opposition from the East Coast. That proved to be a major tactical error on our part.

We first became aware of the BDLF the day after the parade. When Kate got to Trolley Dodgers headquarters that morning, she found that the offices had been ransacked. Papers were everywhere, a water cooler was knocked over, and graffiti was sprayed on the walls. The graffiti was hard to read. It looked like the walls, or the person spraying them, had been shaking when the paint was applied. Just as Kate was dialing the police, she heard a moan coming from behind one of the desks. She grabbed an official Bloomington Trolley Dodgers bat and crept up to the desk. Slowly, she leaned forward to see who was moaning. There on the floor was an elderly man dressed in black. He was holding his lower back with one hand and clutching a royal blue baseball cap with the other.

I arrived shortly after the police and the ambulance. On the west wall, the letters BDLF were painted in bright blue paint. A circle with a slash was now on top of the Bloomington Trolley Dodgers logo.

Paramedics examined the old man. Blue paint covered his index finger. His shirt had been lifted so they could examine his back, and a small tattoo was visible. The tattoo contained the letters BDLF arched over a baseball. It was pretty obvious he had been involved in the vandalism.

Why would a seventy-plus-year-old man want to vandalize this place? And what did "BDLF" mean?

He wouldn't talk to the police, but he did answer the paramedics' questions. They put him on a stretcher and wheeled him out to the ambulance. I asked one of the police officers if he had ever heard of the BDLF. He said he had no idea what it meant.

After the police left, I helped Kate and some of the other workers straighten up the office. Then I went to the newspaper to write the story about the break-in for the next day's paper. I called Major League Baseball to see if they knew what BDLF meant. MLB's public relations director paused for a long time. Then he said something very odd. "It's a myth. They do not exist. Don't waste any more time on this."

"Wait a minute! Who's a myth?"

"There is *no such thing* as the BDLF!"

"What do the letters stand for?"

"That's all I can say. Good-bye."

He hung up. I was on to something. The BDLF. Those letters were sprayed on Trolley Dodgers, Inc.'s walls and tattooed on an old man's back. I filed a brief story describing the break-in and went to the hospital to see if the old man would talk. His room was guarded by a police officer, which made me laugh. Where did they think he was going to go?

I convinced the officer to let me in the room. The old man was awake and watching TV. The Dodgers were playing Atlanta. He seemed to be in much less pain.

"You a cop?" he asked.

"No, I'm a reporter."

"What do you want?" His accent sounded Italian, probably East Coast, I thought.

"Just want to ask you about the break-in. My name is Andy." I offered my hand, and he shook it.

"Vincent. Vincent Artessio is my name. Now why would I talk to you and not my lawyer?"

"Well, it's obvious you were involved. I just thought you might want to explain what BDLF means."

Just then a nurse interrupted us and asked Vincent a few questions. He said he was in pain, so she added some sort of painkiller to his IV. It was just the right concoction to loosen up his tongue, because Vincent started telling me everything. He was the first member of the BDLF to be caught and the first to break the code of silence.

"MLB has known about us for years," he began.

"Us?" I asked.

"The BDLF," he answered. "The Brooklyn Dodgers Liberation Front. The league won't talk about us publicly. If questioned, they deny our existence. People who have talked about us were always lumped in with conspiracy theorists. But the BDLF is real."

"What do you think you can accomplish?"

"We want our Dodgers back," he yelled.

A nurse poked her head in the door.

"It's OK," I told her. "The Dodgers just gave up a double."

"He needs to be resting," she warned. "You can only have a few more minutes."

"Thank you," I said.

Vincent continued. "We're well-financed and well-armed. Mostly because we're all retired and don't have anything better to do. Our sole purpose is to bring the Dodgers back to Brooklyn by any means necessary."

"That sounds like Malcom X," I mumbled.

"Hey, we're racially diverse," he replied. "We just sort of adopted some of the Black Power rhetoric of the sixties.

"For the forty-plus years since the Dodgers left Brooklyn, the BDLF has been playing pranks on the Dodger organization. None of the pranks have been too serious, but we always leave a calling card: a Brooklyn Dodgers hat and a note."

"What does the note usually say?" I asked.

"Give back dem bums," he answered. "Because MLB and the Dodger organization didn't want to acknowledge the existence of the BDLF, most of our activities have gone unreported. A few West Coast reporters know about the pranks, but none would dare suggest it was the work of the BDLF. To do so would mean being ostracized by the East Coast sportswriters. It would be like saying you believed in Big Foot or that Elvis was alive."

I started to feel sympathy for the fans in Brooklyn. I also wondered how much fun the BDLF had over the years pulling these pranks.

"How many members do you have?" I asked.

"There are only three of us left," he said. "The Dodgers left forty years ago. Most of the folks in Brooklyn today never saw the Dodgers play or remember Ebbets Field."

Vincent had come to Bloomington ten days earlier with the other members of the BDLF. Clayton Burkett, an African-American and one of those who embraced the black power rhetoric more strongly than some of the others, believed that "the man" and the commissioner of baseball was the same person. Anthony Lewin was Vincent's other accomplice. Hailing from a predominantly Jewish neighborhood in Brooklyn, Anthony was called Rabbi by Clayton and Vincent. He was an original member of the BDLF, and had masterminded some of the group's greatest pranks.

Few things are able to unite the races in America. However, the love of baseball had kept these three men close friends (and petty criminals) for nearly forty years.

Vincent told me that he, Clayton and Anthony had checked into a Holiday Inn near downtown. They cased headquarters for a few days, learning all the details about the staff, the nearby tenants, and the alley behind the building. In the rush to get Trolley Dodgers, Inc., off the ground, no one had installed an alarm system. It was easy for the three men to break the lock on the back door and enter the offices.

"We busted through about nine o'clock p.m. on the Fourth of July. We started to vandalize the place around ten-thirty."

"What did you do for the first hour and a half?"

"We took a nap. Busting through the door wore us out."

"OK. Then what did you do?"

"I started painting the walls, and the other guys started trashing the place."

"How long did that take?"

"About two hours."

"You only painted BDLF and a circle/slash through the Bloomington logo."

"My hands were shaky. You see how fast you can paint when you get to be seventy-two, smart aleck!"

"Sorry. Please continue."

"Well, I tried to flip over a desk when I finished painting."

"And that's when you hurt your back."

"Yeah, how'd you know?"

"Lucky guess."

"Just when my back gave out, someone pounded on the front door, and the other guys panicked. I couldn't see who was at the door, because I was rolling on the ground in pain. I yelled to the others to go without me, and they did."

He paused for a few moments. I was writing down notes as quickly as possible. I didn't speak.

Finally he spoke. “I didn’t mean it.”

“Mean what?”

He hesitated again. “Go on without me. It’s just something guys say in the movies. But they never leave the person. Or if they do, they always come back. Why didn’t they come back?”

“I don’t know. Would you like me to go look for them?”

“You’re not going to turn them in, are you?”

“No, Vincent. I promise.”

I felt sad for him as I left. There was hurt in his eyes when he said, “Why didn’t they come back?” These had been his pals for fifty years. Why didn’t they come back? Maybe they tried. I had to find out.

As I walked to my car, I started thinking about why I wasn’t angry with the BDLF guys for what they did to the office. I knew it was because if Darryl, Klondike and I had lived in Brooklyn in the fifties, we would have been the BDLF. It also made me realize that three guys like us in Los Angeles were probably considering the same type of organization if the Dodgers moved to Bloomington. The part of me that felt bad for Los Angeles fans was at war with the part of me that felt they had stolen the team. We’re stealing it back.

My cell phone rang. “Hello.”

“We found teeth.”

“Who is this?”

“It’s Kate. We found teeth at the crime scene.”

“Congratulations! Save me one; I’ll make a necklace.”

“They’re dentures.”

“Hmmm . . . in that case, I’ll need a bigger chain. Will you continue to see me socially if I wear dentures around my neck?”

“No way. People look at me weird enough already when I’m with you.”

“Coward. Did you tell the police about the dentures?”

“Not yet.”

“Good. Don’t call them. I’m on my way.”

I picked up the dentures at headquarters and drove to the Holiday Inn. There was a "Do Not Disturb" sign on the doorknob, but I knocked anyway. No answer. I kept knocking.

"Go away."

"I have your teeth."

Long pause. I could hear Anthony and Clayton arguing.

"Slide them under the door."

I looked at the teeth. I looked at the door.

"You're kidding, right?"

Long pause. "Set them down and go away."

"I just came from the hospital and I talked to Vincent. I'm not going to turn you in, but I want to talk to you. I know about the BDLF."

Long pause. "What's the BDLF?"

"Brooklyn Dodgers Liberation Front." I had barely gotten the words out when the door opened and a large hand grabbed my shirt, pulling me into the dark hotel room. The door slammed behind me and I stumbled face first onto the bed.

It took me a second to get past the shock of being thrown onto the bed. I rolled over and standing before me were two elderly gentlemen. One was a black man with grey hair. He was bald down the center of his head. The two grey puffs on either side looked like clouds around a mountain peak. He was holding a baseball bat.

Next to him was a white elderly gentleman who also had grey hair on either side of a bald patch. His white dress shirt was unbuttoned, revealing a stained tank undershirt and a Star of David hanging from a gold chain.

"What do you want, cracker?" said the man with the bat.

"Where are my teeth?" gummed the other.

I held out Anthony's teeth and he snatched them from me. Slowly, he walked to the bathroom.

"I just wanted to bring you the teeth, and find out what happened. Why didn't you go back for Vincent?"

"Vincent? How do you know Vincent?" Clayton said. He was still holding the bat and standing over me.

"I just met him in the hospital."

"Vincent's in the hospital? We got to get back to New York." He yelled to Anthony, "Hey, Rabbi! We got to get back to Brooklyn! Vincent's in the hospital."

"Again, with the yelling? I'm right here." He came back from the bathroom, teeth in place. "Vincent's in the hospital?"

"I don't think you guys understand. Vincent's in the hospital here, in Bloomington."

"Vincent's here? Why is he here?" Anthony asked.

"You broke into the Trolley Dodgers headquarters together. Remember, you lost your teeth."

"You better start making sense, white boy. Or else I will beat the truth out of you by any means necessary." Clayton pulled back with the bat like he was going to take a swing at me.

It was at this point that I realized that Vincent wasn't abandoned by his mates. Their minds had been abandoned by time. Senility is the bane of any gang of vandals. I was going to have to convince Anthony and Clayton that they had left Vincent behind.

"Guys, ten days ago you came from Brooklyn to Bloomington," I began. "Vincent was with you. You tried to vandalize the headquarters of Trolley Dodgers, Inc." I paused. "You left Vincent behind."

Clayton sat down on the bed, visibly shaking. "I remember now."

"You know about the BDLF," Anthony asked. "Are we going to jail?"

"No, you're not going to jail," I answered. "Why don't you let me take you to Vincent? I think he would really like to see you both."

I called Kate and convinced her to drop the charges. Then I drove the two men to the hospital. Upon reuniting, each man shed a few tears. They were fully aware that their bodies had betrayed them years ago. But now they were confronted with the deterioration of their minds. They agreed that they needed to start looking after each other.

After a long silence, I tried to break the tension. "So," I asked, "tell me what it was like to watch Jackie Robinson." That's all it took. Double-headers and pennant races washed away the tears. Recollections of sunny days in Brooklyn replaced the pain of growing old.

Ah, the stories. Jackie's first game in Ebbets Field was followed by a double-play story involving Pee Wee Reese. Clayton caught a home run ball hit by Duke Snyder. There were World Series games against the Yankees and pennant battles with the Giants. Road trips to the Polo Grounds and games listened to on the radio. Their stories wove a rich tapestry of New York baseball.

They talked until the nurse kicked us out. I drove them back to their hotel, and offered to meet them for breakfast. I couldn't get enough of the old baseball stories.

"Do you think you're done with baseball terrorism?"

"Yeah, I guess we better retire," Anthony said.

"You know, we're not the ones who took the Dodgers away from Brooklyn. It was the McGuires. We're just bringing them halfway back to Brooklyn. It seems to me you should pull one last prank on a member of the McGuire family. You know, a last hurrah."

"I'm too tired to go to L.A.," Anthony said. "I think we're done."

"You don't have to go to L.A. There's a member of their family right here in Bloomington."

"Really?" Clayton said. "What's his name?"

I smiled, turned to Clayton and said, "Frank Wolf."

SIXTEEN

Waiting for Oprah

(Money Raised: $94,345,623.35)

"I feel greatly honored to have a ballpark named after me, especially since I've been thrown out of so many."

~ *Casey Stengel*

THE FOLLOWING MONDAY, I found myself in the Scarlet Cricket parked outside the Bloomington Convention Center. Klondike sat next to me, while Darryl was stretched out in the back seat. We had been sitting there for a while. No one spoke and no one reached for his door handle. Each man was waiting for the other to say we were backing out. This was uncharted territory. It was the night we had to make good on our promise to attend a Mary Kay meeting. If I had any hope of continuing my relationship with Kate, I had to be a man of my word.

"Let's do this," I said and threw open my door.

"Do you think somebody famous is coming to this meeting?" Klondike asked. "I've never seen so many cars in the parking lot before, and Kate said there would be a guest speaker."

"Maybe it's the First Lady," Darryl said.

"Maybe Oprah is coming!" said Klondike. "With this many cars, it's got to be Oprah."

We found Kate just inside the lobby. She had been too busy to join us for dinner before the meeting.

"You guys are late, just as I suspected," she scolded us. "You've probably been sitting in your car trying to muster up the courage to come in, haven't you?"

How did she know? I thought.

"How did you know?" Klondike said out loud. Darryl and I both shoved him.

"You're terribly predictable," she answered. "Follow me."

Kate pushed open the double doors to the convention hall. Trailing behind her were three very nervous men. Although only a handful of women turned to see Darryl, Klondike, and me enter, it felt like everyone in the room was staring at me. I wanted to shout, "I'm not here for a makeover."

"Everybody is staring at us," Klondike whispered.

"That's because your fly is open," Darryl said. Klondike looked down to check his zipper and then muttered a curse at Darryl. Kate wheeled around and gave us the mom look. You know the one. The look a mom can give you that says, "If you embarrass me, your bodies will never be found." We stopped talking.

What we were about to witness was the equivalent of a Monday Night Football game for the Mary Kay world. A capacity crowd filled the main hall of the Convention Center. It had the buzz of Oscar night. Maybe Oprah *was* coming. Four hundred sharply dressed women and three men with visible sweat beads on their foreheads sat waiting for Oprah. As the excitement continued to grow, women in blue coats, red coats, and pink coats were busy welcoming new consultants to the event. They directed people to their seats and passed out little pink bags. Nobody handed me a pink bag. I was relieved.

The excited chatter came to a fever pitch, and then a woman in her late forties made her way to the podium. This was it. She was going to introduce Oprah, I was sure of it.

"What's about to happen?" Darryl asked.

"I think Oprah must be here," I said.

"Oprah? I'm going to get her autograph," Klondike shouted with glee.

He was sitting between the two of us, so both Darryl and I grabbed him and pulled him back into his chair. "You're not going to go hound Oprah. She probably has bodyguards," Darryl warned. "Besides, if she's going to sign autographs, she's going to sign for the ladies first."

Klondike leaned back and began to mope. "It's not fair. Why do the Mary Kay ladies get all the autographs?"

At this point I couldn't have cared if Pete Rose was going to speak. All I could think was, somebody please start this so these women will stop staring at me. Of course, nobody really was staring at me.

The lady at the podium introduced herself as Karen Kincaid. She had been a Mary Kay consultant for more than ten years. She wore a turquoise suit. Apparently the turquoise ladies were higher-ranking officers. She then went on to introduce the night's featured speaker.

"Coming to the podium in a minute is a woman who had her humble beginnings in Oak Ridge, Tennessee. She was a single mom, living in a trailer park."

It was at this point that I began to be skeptical about Oprah making an appearance.

"On a cold, rainy night in November of 1983, she attended a makeover party at her cousin Francine's house."

"Klondike, does Oprah have a cousin named Francine?" I asked.

"Huh?" Klondike seemed annoyed that I interrupted the introduction.

Karen continued. "That night she was introduced to a new way of living. A new way of supporting herself. A new way of achieving her dreams. She went home that night and made a list of people who might be able to loan her money. She borrowed some money and purchased a starter kit. Eighteen months later she was handed the keys to her first new car: a shiny, yellow Oldsmobile Firenza."

She definitely was not talking about Oprah. However, the person she was describing turned out to be every bit as entertaining. I noticed that Klondike was on the edge of his seat. Darryl had stretched his legs out, his feet almost touching the feet of the lady sitting in front of him. I was the only one who still had sweat beads.

"Today, she earns an average of $750,000 per year and lives in a multimillion-dollar home in Louisville, Kentucky. She has sponsored more than seventy-five directors and has been the keynote speaker at annual conventions for IBM, Microsoft, and Pepsi-Cola. Please welcome the lovely Ms. Emily Davis."

All four hundred women shot to their feet in applause and cheers. Klondike jumped up, too. Darryl and I stared at him in amazement for a good ten seconds before we realized we were the only ones in the room who were still seated. I quickly got up and clapped. Darryl kind of stumbled trying to get his long legs out from under the seat in front of him. He didn't miss much of the ovation because it went on for what seemed like five minutes.

Finally, everyone took their seats and Emily began her speech. It didn't take long to see why she was so successful. Her delivery was polished and professional, but a gentle southern accent softened her presentation. She was Donald Trump, Knute Rockne, and a Southern Baptist minister in a business suit and heels.

She started with a more in-depth account of her life. "I was working at a grocery store when I became a Mary Kay consultant. My first two months produced little results, but I kept at it whenever I had spare time.

"My first big break came when I did a few makeovers for a sorority homecoming dance at the University of Tennessee in Knoxville. I had so much repeat business from girls at the university that I moved from Oak Ridge to Knoxville."

The brilliance in her speech was in the way she constantly pulled the listeners into her story. Her voice was a warm southern breeze that gently picked you up and carried you away to where her story took place. Her story was real. It had pain and it had setbacks. The narrative did not always contain success, but it always contained hope. It became quickly evident that this was not a get-rich-quick culture. This was an empowering culture. A culture that said you can turn your life around. You can take control of your life. It was a culture that was devoid of the cynicism and doubt that had plagued me most of my life.

Although it was very inspiring, her speech did have a drawback. Klondike, Darryl, and I began to lose ourselves in the moment. By the time she was finished, I was convinced that *I* could sell lipstick. And Klondike, well, let's just say Emily had a profound impact on his soul. When she called for responses from the crowd, we began to respond too. At the end of her speech, she gave an invitation for guests to come to the front if they wanted to become part of the company. Unfortunately, Klondike had been whipped into a fury by this point. When the invitation came, he stood up.

He got nearly a step and a half away before Darryl was able to grab his arm. He yanked on him hard enough to cause Klondike to fall back into his seat. Because we were sitting against the side wall, his head hit with a loud thud. To make matters worse, the wall was actually a partition dividing the massive conference hall. Not being a solid wall, the impact caused it to shudder enough to get the attention of everyone else sitting against the wall.

Klondike moaned for a few seconds, and then began to squirm like a four-year-old. Darryl refused to let go. "What are you doing? *You're a man!*" said Darryl in an aggravated whisper.

"Let me go, I want to sign Bonnie up."

"What? You can't sign your wife up for this." I said. "She has to *want* to do it."

Klondike was able to squirm hard enough to break Darryl's grip. However, his momentum caused him to fall off his chair. He lay motionless for a few seconds as he tried to get his bearings. The pause was all Darryl needed. He jumped from his chair on top of Klondike. "You're *not* going up there."

"Let me go. I want to change my life—I mean Bonnie's life."

They began to wrestle on the floor like two little kids. The sweat beads had returned to my forehead. Fortunately most of the women were focused on what was going on up front. Only about twenty were watching the wrestling match in the back corner of the room. Klondike was flailing all over the place, bumping into chairs, tables, and guests. He had almost freed himself when Kate came back into the room.

The usually composed, graceful Kate underwent a metamorphosis at that moment. The mom look came back, but this one was different. She gave me the kind of look that a wife gives her husband when she finds the children doing something really bad and her husband has made absolutely no effort to put an end to their behavior.

She quickly rushed to Klondike and Darryl and picked them up by their ears. Both of them howled in pain as she dragged them out the closest door into the lobby of the hotel. I remember thinking that my two best friends were about to die. And I remember not having the courage to try to save them. I also remember the rest of the ladies staring at me. As far as the eye could see, there were women giving me the "wait till your father gets home" look.

I waited inside for a really long time. When I finally got the courage to walk out, Klondike and Darryl were sitting back to back on two chairs in the lobby. Both of them stared at the ground. Kate didn't seem to be around. I quickly walked over to the sulking children and said, "Let's get out of here fast."

"You're not going anywhere," hissed the mom voice over my shoulder. My shoulders shrank. I was busted. "You boys are going to help clean up after all the ladies have left. I think it's the least you could do for embarrassing me tonight."

"But I didn't even . . ." was all I was able to get out.

"I don't want to hear it," she said. "Sit down across from them until I come back for you. Any lip from you three and I'll demote you to hot dog vendors at the new ballpark." She turned and headed outside.

It was at this point that I became aware of a commotion in the parking lot. Through the lobby window, I could see a TV truck with spotlights shining on a group of people carrying signs. The DWARVES were outside! They were protesting animal testing.

Now, for the record, I'm not against cosmetic testing on animals in certain instances. For example, I think a little lipstick and eye shadow might make a female hippopotamus feel a little less bitter about looking like—um—a female hippopotamus. But that's just my opinion and I'm often wrong. However, Mary Kay doesn't test its products on animals, so the DWARVES were very misinformed.

Kate headed straight for the protesters. Klondike, Darryl and I jumped up and ran through the revolving door to save her from being torn to pieces. But we stopped short on the sidewalk. She seemed to be completely in control of the situation. She confidently made her way to the reporter through a chorus of boos. Before the reporter could ask her first question, Maple demanded, "How many innocent animals have been killed in the laboratories of your make-up empire?"

"None, and I can say no guilty ones have been killed either," Kate replied.

Maple didn't get the joke. "Liar!" she screamed.

So Kate directed her next response towards the reporter. "Our company recognizes our responsibility to be good neighbors to both people and animals. That's why we haven't tested on animals since the late eighties and will continue to look for environmentally friendly ways to do business."

"You're telling me that you haven't used animal testing for more than eight years?" asked the reporter.

"Yes, that's correct," Kate replied.

The reporter made a neck-slashing signal to the cameraman. He lowered his camera and turned off the spotlight from the news van. "This isn't news," she said to her cameraman. "We're out of here."

The dejected and slightly embarrassed DWARVES lowered their signs and quietly left the convention center parking lot.

Maple didn't leave right away. She and Kate had a long one-on-one conversation. When they were done, Maple smiled and walked away. I had never seen Maple smile. Kate crossed over the unloading zone towards the front door of the convention center. She looked pleased with herself, until she saw Klondike, Darryl and I watching from the sidewalk.

"I thought I told you guys to stay put until I was ready for you."

We ran to the revolving door and pushed our way inside. All three of us were jammed into one space trying desperately to get back to our seats in the lobby. We pushed so hard on the revolving door that when we came around to the opening, Klondike went face first onto the lobby carpet. Darryl landed on Klondike, and I landed on Darryl. Unfortunately, I didn't quite get my legs out of the door before someone pushed the door around. It jammed on my ankle, causing the person to repeatedly shove the door, each time a little harder. He must have been hard of hearing or really dimwitted because he never made the connection that each time he pushed, a loud painful scream erupted from deep inside me.

Darryl managed to pull me free and help me stand. He then helped me limp to my chair. I looked at Klondike. His forehead bore a maple-leaf-shaped rug burn from the lobby carpet. A few minutes later, Kate returned and put us to work. We helped stack chairs and clear tables. After an hour of work, Kate dismissed us. I still had a limp from the revolving door and Klondike's rug burn hadn't gone away. Despite being mad at us, she gave Klondike a sample bag for his wife and daughters. She also had a goody bag for Darryl's wife. She gave me, on the other hand, a bag of trash and told me to throw it in the dumpster on my way out. I was in the doghouse, and this one was painted pink.

SEVENTEEN

Sunday Drive

(Money Raised: $99,775,423.35)

"How old would you be if you didn't know how old you are?"

~ *Satchel Paige*

BY SUNDAY, KATE WAS SPEAKING to me again. And by the following Monday, she was letting me speak back. In late July, the Bloomington Speedway hosted a race to benefit children with cancer. Local businesses put up the prize money and all the evening's proceeds went to the cancer ward at Riley Children's Hospital in Indianapolis.

I convinced Kate and the Trolley Dodgers' board to put up the money to enter a car in the race.

"It shows that we're willing to give back to the community from the very beginning," I explained. "I also know of a driver who's better than Jeff Gordon and Steve Kinser combined."

We were a late entry, but the race organizers let us in since the proceeds were for charity. The race was to be a thirty-five-lap final with one preliminary heat and a qualifying round. The rules would be the same as the World of Outlaws tour that had a stop in Bloomington. But anyone with a sprint car who made the deadline could enter.

Convincing the board and getting a late entry were the first hurdles. Now, we needed a car. Klondike had a buddy named

Derek who loved to work on cars. He had been a crew chief on the sprint car circuit and always had a few race cars around his shop that he tinkered with. He agreed to supply us with a car and to serve as our crew chief.

"You're also going to have to be the crew," I told him.

"What do you mean?"

"We don't have anybody that knows anything about cars," I answered.

"I see. Don't worry about it. I'll get some people together. What about a driver?"

"Oh, we have a driver," I answered. "I'll have him out at the track on Wednesday if you think you can have the car ready."

"Yeah, I can do that."

"Thanks, I'll see you then."

On Wednesday afternoon, Derek arrived, towing the car on a trailer. He got out, shook my hand and I introduced him to my driver. "This is . . . uh . . . Rodney."

Derek looked very suspiciously at Rodney—mostly because Rodney was wearing his helmet with the visor down. He didn't speak to Derek, just shook his hand and nodded. Derek walked to his trailer turning back to look at Rodney several times.

He put down the gate on the trailer and drove the car off the back. Leaving it running, he got out and walked towards us. "She's all yours. Give her a try."

With that, Rodney climbed awkwardly into the car and strapped himself in. Derek looked at me like he was puzzled.

"Where did you find this guy?"

"Oh, he's been driving for years."

"How come I've never heard of him?"

"He's . . . uh . . . new to the Midwest."

Rodney peeled out of the parking lot and made his way onto the dirt oval. "It will take him a couple of laps to warm up," I said, "but time him anyway."

Seventeen seconds later Rodney zoomed by us. Fifteen seconds later he drove by again. On his third lap, he was back in thirteen seconds. Derek had the gleam of a child at Christmas in his eye when he looked up from his stopwatch. "We're gonna win! We're gonna win!"

Rodney drove six or seven laps, then pulled the car off the track and drove back to the trailer. We helped him out and he waved and walked to the parking lot, got in his car and left, never removing his helmet. Derek followed him, staring in disbelief.

"He had another appointment to get to."

"Why didn't he take his helmet off?"

"Superstitious maybe?" I was reaching.

"Wait a minute. You went up to Indy and got an Andretti, didn't you?"

"No, I swear. That's not an Andretti!"

"I'll bet that's John Andretti or Michael!"

"Derek, I swear that was *not* an Andretti!"

"Well, something's fishy about that driver."

"But can he drive?"

"Yes, better than anybody I've ever seen at this track."

"Good. That's all you need to know."

On race day, Derek was even more suspicious. Rodney didn't speak or take off his helmet during any of the pre-race activities or drivers' briefing. Even the other drivers were curious. It took a lot of reassuring to convince Derek that everything would be OK, and that it definitely was *not* an Andretti.

Rodney took a few practice laps and seemed to be comfortable in the car. Tonight's race was between open wheel sprint cars. On top of each car is a funny-looking wing that keeps the cars from getting airborne or rolling through the turns. Derek had painted the wing Dodger blue and gave it the number 42 in honor of Jackie Robinson. On the side of the car were our logo and phone number.

During qualifications, Rodney showed a glimpse of greatness. His second lap was just under thirteen seconds, close to the track record. The evening was set up with two preliminary heats of twelve cars each. This was followed by a Trophy Dash, in which the top cars from the preliminary heats competed to improve their position in the A Main Event. The bottom finishers from the first races competed in the B Main Event, with the top four finishers moving on. The A Main Event would have sixteen cars racing for the grand prize. Normally, this would be a cash prize. However, since tonight's event was for charity, they were simply competing for a trophy.

Rodney led the preliminary heat for the first eight laps. But on lap nine, he came upon a car that was struggling with its set-up. They entered the third turn wide, leaving Rodney room to pass. But just as Rodney ducked under to pass him, the slower car closed in and hit the Trolley Dodger car. The collision caused Rodney's car to roll and sent him over the high outside bank and down to the grass below.

I freaked out, running through the infield, across the track and over the high bank. When I got to the car, Rodney signaled that he was OK. A truck towed the car back to the infield and Derek quickly went to work. The wing was badly damaged. We didn't have a replacement, so Derek bent and straightened it the best he could. Rodney would have to win the B Main event, or at least finish in the top four to have a chance at the big race.

With the patched-up car, Rodney managed to barely finish fourth to qualify for the A Main Event. But he did so with style, passing five cars on the final lap to finish the race. Then he pulled into the infield to let Derek set the car up for the final race. Up till then, Rodney had communicated with hand gestures or through me.

Rodney flipped up his mask. "The pitch and the stagger aren't right."

"I have no idea what you're talking about," I answered. "You better talk to Derek."

Now, he opened his visor slightly and barked out orders. When he first spoke, Derek took a step back and fell over his tools. He looked over at me in complete bewilderment. It took him at least a minute to respond or even get up. Finally he started laughing and rose to his feet.

Following Rodney's orders, he tweaked the wing pitch and position quickly and adjusted the stagger on the right rear wheel. When he was done, he gave Rodney a thumbs-up and watched him make his way onto the track. I made my way back to the stands to watch the race with Kate.

"If we win this race, we're going to double our investors in a week," I said.

"What are you talking about?" she asked.

"Trust me, this is going to put us back on page one. At least for a few days."

"It's a sprint car race. I think you're exaggerating the exposure we're getting. If we had an entry at the Brickyard, then I might agree with you."

I winced at the mention of the Brickyard.

"Sorry," she said. "If it makes you feel better, I promise never to leave you for a Pit Boy. Formula One driver, maybe. But never for a Pit Boy."

"Swell. Just watch the race. And stay away from the drivers."

Sixteen cars roared past at the start of the final race. The Trolley Dodgers entry started in last place, with twenty laps to pass the other cars. After two laps, he was in tenth. After ten laps, he was in second. On the fourteenth lap, Rodney passed local racing legend Steve Kinser. By the time the white flag came out, he was seven car lengths ahead of second place. This time there would be no crash on the final lap. The Trolley Dodgers car had won. He crossed the finish line with a hand raised to the crowd. Then, he pulled into the winner's circle and Derek helped him out of the car. He and Derek each held a side of the trophy over their heads. As they lowered it, Rodney finally took off his helmet. The five thousand fans who had crowded into the Bloomington Speedway that night gasped as one. I alone stood and cheered and clapped. Kate quickly regained her composure and stood and clapped. Slowly, the people around her got up, one by one. Minutes later, everyone was cheering.

A tear ran down Roxy's cheek as she stood next to the car waving to the crowd. That day Roxy Bennett became the oldest person and first female to win a race at the Bloomington Speedway. It was her seventy-second birthday.

EIGHTEEN

Insults and Injury at Noble Bush Field

(Money Raised: $125,118,593.35)

"Sometimes reporters write what I say and not what I mean."
~ *Pedro Guerrero*

SEVERAL DAYS LATER I WAS still on a high from Roxy's big racing win. Ira assigned me to cover an invitational baseball tournament being held at Winslow Sports Complex. Bloomington's Babe Ruth League All Stars were playing a team from Rushville, Indiana. I called Kate to see if she would like to go along. She was excited about going until she realized that I was picking her up in my not-so-new Pacer.

The Scarlet Cricket had died. The guy who towed it for me said that in forty years in the wrecker business, he had never seen an engine block fall completely out of a car. The Pacer had arrived from Indianapolis several weeks before and had been in the shop since. I picked it up the same day the Cricket expired.

Kate was, shall we say, less than enthusiastic to be picked up in a Pacer. The bright yellow paint and the fish bowl windows didn't help. It looked like a yellow submarine. I decided I would need to keep a Beatles CD in the car at all times.

"You're not taking me anywhere in that thing."

"You drive a pink Cadillac. It isn't any less of a head-turner than this car."

"But my car is a *Cadillac*. Get it? It's a Caddy. People like Caddies. People envy Caddies. People *laugh* at Pacers."

"They do?"

"Yes, they do."

I paused for a moment. "Are you sure they don't envy Pacers?"

"Nobody envies a Pacer. Trust me."

"OK. We'll take your car," I agreed. Hoping for a change of heart I added, "It has vinyl seats."

"Don't care," she muttered and walked towards the Cadillac.

"I took out the eight-track and put in a CD player."

"Don't care," she shouted as she opened her door.

"His and her cup holders."

"Still don't care. Are you getting in, because I'm leaving," she shouted while she started the Cadillac.

I abandoned the Yellow Submarine and sat down in the Cadillac. "OK, I'll admit that the Cadillac is nicer than the Pacer." She gave me the "duh" look. I hate it when I get the "duh" look. "But the Pacer has character," I added. She rolled her eyes.

When we arrived at the park, I immediately realized that this would be an entertaining evening because The Wolf's van was parked up on the sidewalk close to one of the fields. A first-class jerk can create first-class headlines. Tonight would be no exception.

Also in attendance was a contingent of DWARVES. They were raising money to help educate people about the environmental impact of a proposed highway extension. They were also soliciting help to locate The Ten. Since I felt somewhat responsible for their disappearance, I stopped at their table and gave a donation. Maple looked at me very suspiciously. She looked different, but I couldn't quite put my finger on why.

"What are you up to? You've never supported us before."

"Believe it or not, I actually support many of the causes you do. I just like to have a steak once in a while."

"Well, I do have to admit that I was surprised that you're going to honor the DWARVES at Gomez Park. I was even more surprised that you were going to have vegetarian concession stands. Thanks." Maple smiled.

"You're welcome. Maybe this baseball thing can help bring together a lot of people who haven't gotten along in the past." I grabbed a couple of "Support DWARVES" bumper stickers.

"Maybe. Just try to find an alternative to wood bats, OK?"

"I'll see what I can do. Good luck finding The Ten."

"Thanks."

I left Maple and caught up with Kate, who was talking to some friends near The Wolf's van. The Wolf was seated in the dugout, barking out instructions to his wife, kids, and the players on his team. The kids were pulling equipment out from the side door of the van and his wife was in the driver's seat waiting to move it back to the parking lot. I used Kate's body as a shield to put a DWARVES bumper sticker on the back of their van.

Kate said goodbye to her friends, and we continued towards the bleachers. As we walked past the front of the van, The Wolf saw me from the dugout. He snarled at me. I smiled, waved and then made a motion like I was lifting an imaginary skirt so he could see my leg. I love taunting The Wolf.

"I saw you talking to Maple," Kate said. "Were you being nice?"

"Yes, and so was she," I answered. "And guess what? I think she was wearing make-up."

"Really? Imagine that . . ." Her voice sort of trailed off. She was up to something, I was sure of it. Maybe this had something to do with their conversation at the convention center. I tried to get more information from her, but she wouldn't talk. So my attention turned back to the field.

The Wolf managed to elicit hate from the umpires before the first pitch. He complained that the other team had more infield practice time than his team. Suffering from small man's disease, The Wolf tried to compensate by being boisterous and overly aggressive. So he just marched his team out to the field before the other team had finished their infield drills. He was yelling at the umps, trying to "mark his territory" but paying no attention to the other team.

The Rushville coach yelled to the second baseman to throw home. And, being the disciplined athlete that he was, he did just that. It was hardly his fault that The Wolf was walking onto the field, or that the ball met The Wolf just above his temple. The impact stopped The Wolf dead in his tracks, opening up a one-inch gash in his head. He came to after about twenty to thirty seconds (too short a time for my taste) and proceeded to threaten a lawsuit on anyone within a five-mile radius of the park. That's when I noticed our photographer had gone onto the field and was taking close-up shots. He threatened to sue her as well.

Mrs. Wolf backed the van up to the field and with the help of the assistant coaches managed to get The Wolf inside. She drove off rather hastily, and we turned our attention to the game.

Now you would think that a head injury would make this a Wolf-free game. It didn't. He came back with a white gauze headband, the perfect accessory for the bloody T-shirt he had failed to change before he came back. The injury hadn't subdued his anger; it had intensified it.

His team was down by five runs when he returned. They were in the field and runners were on first and third. The pitcher (his son) threw a wild pitch. The ball hit the backstop, took a weird bounce and rolled almost to the visitors' dugout. By the time the catcher got to the ball, the runner on third had scored, and the runner on first had made it all the way to third. Now The Wolf was furious. Yelling at his son, he kicked the bats off the bat rack in his dugout.

The next pitch hit the plate and the runner started down the line to first. The Wolf tore out of the dugout, screaming at the umpire for not calling a strike. However, he tripped on one of the bats that he had just kicked and fell forward to his knees. That was the last straw. He got up with a vein bulging in his neck, on a mission to give the umpire a piece of his mind. "A piece" is about all he was able to give. The ump ejected him before he got the first sentence out, causing what little composure The Wolf had left to evaporate into the July evening sky.

The Wolf's assistant coaches had to carry him off the field. Officials from the Winslow Sports Complex threatened to banish him from all tournaments and league play.

After the game, I lost track of Kate on the way out. I found her talking to Maple. They were laughing pretty hard about something. When I got close, Kate said goodbye and walked away from the table.

"What were you two laughing about?" I asked.

"Your car."

"The Pacer? You're both jealous of that car."

"She also mentioned the time she hit you in the head with a cafeteria tray."

"And you thought that was funny?"

"Absolutely."

"I'm glad you can revel in my pain. Just take me to my Yellow Submarine. At least it won't make fun of me."

"Or start."

"Funny. You know, Summer Fest is next weekend. The BoDeans are playing."

"Now, I would actually ride in the Pacer to see them."

"Really?"

"No, you're leaving the Pacer home," she answered. "But, we *are* going to the concert."

NINETEEN

Good Things

(Money Raised: $134,687,893.35)

"To live and die it seems, is a waste without a dream."
~ *BoDeans*

THE BLOOMINGTON SUMMER FEST is held every year at the Showers Plaza parking lot. It runs Friday and Saturday and features live music, local food vendors, a beer garden, and artist craft booths. The grand finale is the Saturday night concert. We were really excited this year because the headline act was the BoDeans. Hailing from Waukesha, Wisconsin, the BoDeans were highly popular in Bloomington. The band was made up of Kurt Neumann, Sam Llannas, Bobby Griffin, and Nick Kitsos on drums. Occasionally, local music legend Kenny Aronoff would play with the band. Their single "Good Things" was written in Bloomington and still got a lot of local radio airplay. This happened to be the first time back to Summer Fest for the band. They had played many shows around town over the years, but this was the first Summer Fest show since an infamous late eighties show.

That year, the Summer Fest was held in the downtown parking garage. The organizers had grossly underestimated the popularity of the band. When it came time to take the stage, more than three thousand people were crammed on the top deck of the garage. Just a few songs into the show, the police shut the concert down because the floor of the garage was moving. Some of the more intoxicated fans got a little rowdy. After that, it took a long time to get the Summer Fest people to bring back the BoDeans. It wasn't the band's fault. The city had just been unprepared. At any rate, the event was moved to the Showers site in the mid-nineties. A former furniture factory, it had been renovated and now housed city government offices and the Indiana University research park. At this new location, there was more room for vendors, and the ground wouldn't move.

Kate and I arrived in the late afternoon. I wasn't allowed to drive the Submarine. The BoDeans wouldn't be taking the stage for a few hours, so we had time to eat and check out some of the arts and crafts booths. We were sitting at a table, feasting on some ribs, when I spotted Pete in the distance. He had a date for the evening, and as they came closer, moving from booth to booth, I slowly could observe more of her appearance. She was a lot younger than Pete, probably mid-twenties to his early forties. Something was strangely familiar about her.

Kate poked me in the arm and pointed to the couple. "What do you think about Pete's date?"

"She's a lot younger than Pete. Maybe it's a mid-life crisis thing."

"No, I think they have a lot in common, despite their age difference."

"How would you know?" I asked.

"Well for one, Pete is my boss, right?"

"Yes and . . ." I answered.

"And, I gave the girl a makeover earlier today," she replied.

"Really. What's her name?"

"Her real name is Martha Sullivan," Kate said. "You probably know her better as Maple."

I spit beer all over my ribs. "What? You can't be serious."

"I am serious. And, could you not spray beer all over *my* ribs?"

"Pete and Maple?"

"*Martha*," she said.

"Right, Martha. Pete and Martha."

I rested my head in my hands. "I'm so confused. The earth is going to crash into the sun. I'm sure of it. What's next? The Wolf is elected president?"

Kate tried to console me. "There, there. The earth is not going to crash into the sun. But you may be in for some changes and that's a good thing. I think you and Maple—"

I raised my head and cut her off. "*Martha*."

"Right, Martha." She continued, "I think you and Martha are going to find some common ground once you get to know each other. The political left and the political right becoming friends. It will be great."

"But I'm not on the political right. Why does everybody assume that?"

"Where *are* you then?"

"I consider myself politically agnostic."

"What does that mean?"

"It means I refuse to choose sides because the day I turn thirty-five, I'm running for president as an independent."

"Even *I* wouldn't vote for you," she said.

"Seriously, though, there aren't enough people that recognize that neither the right nor the left has a corner on truth."

"So you're a centrist?" she asked.

"No, I'm pretty much a Freddy."

At just that moment, Pete and Martha walked up. "You have rib sauce on your forehead," Pete said.

"Thanks for letting me know. Some people would have let me walk around with it all night." I glared at Kate.

As I wiped the sauce off my head, Pete introduced his date, "Martha." After some awkward chitchat, they made their way to the beer tent. I just shook my head. "Be nice," Kate ordered.

"I wasn't going to say anything. I just can't imagine how those two got together."

"How did *we* get together?" she asked.

"You fell in a moment of weakness."

"Really?"

"And, I've been beaming subliminal messages into your home while you sleep."

She leaned over and kissed me. "It's working."

Pete and Martha returned with beer and food and we sat with them while they ate. As they did, the crowd started to build for the main event. About three thousand people had squeezed in between the stage and the food tables and vendors. They were starting to become impatient for the show to start when finally a local radio personality took the stage. After thanking various sponsors he shouted, "And now from Waukesha, Wisconsin, the band some of you have waited all day for: the BoDeans!"

Lights dimmed. The drums rolled. And two unmistakable guitars lit into the song "Naked." I didn't have to be a reporter or a PR director for Trolley Dodgers, Inc., for the next two hours. I just had to breathe, laugh and sing. Oh, and dance because Kate grabbed my hand and started wedging her way through the crowd towards the stage. We found a somewhat comfortable place only seven feet from the stage. I gulped the last of my beer—most had been spilled while cutting through the crowd—and let my cup fall to the pavement. That hand was needed to go around Kate's waist when the band broke out an old, slow favorite: "Pick Up the Pieces."

We slow-danced, her in front and me gently swaying her from behind. My mind wandered for a minute until the roar of the crowd brought me back to the show. The intro to the next song energized the crowd and people started jumping up and down in rhythm with the drums. "One, two, three, four!" yelled Kurt. Guitars and screams blended together, filling the midsummer air with "Texas Ride Songs." You could barely hear the band because the crowd was singing every word.

"I found a love, sweet and young, out in the big open," Kate sang at the top of her lungs. "Deep in the land of stars that shine, bright like the heart she wore."

Three thousand fans answered back, "Let's go, shall we? On through the majesty. Let's go, you never know, this was made for you and me."

What followed was a romp through Texas with the band and the crowd clapping, singing, and dancing. By the end of the song, we were dripping with sweat. I made a drinking motion with my hands and she nodded in agreement. We made our way through the crowd. As we walked they played an acoustic version of "True Devotion." The counter melody, always supplied by the BoDeans fans, echoed in our ears, seeming to hang in the trees as we got in line at the beer tent. After a quick trip to the restrooms we were on our way back through the crowds. This time we saw Darryl and his wife Melissa, who followed us back through the crowd. Just as we arrived, a large group of fans made a dash for the restroom, leaving a huge opening for us. We arrived just in time for the band to play "Good Work." It must have been one of Kate's favorites because she completely let loose. She was so into it that she was dancing in her own little world. One of the guys running the lights for the band put a spotlight on her. Kurt, Sammy, and Bobby all slowly gravitated towards her as they continued to play the song.

She suddenly realized that the band and most of the fans near the stage were looking at her. She just smiled, turned only mildly red and kept dancing. Just then, I remembered all over again how very breathtaking she was. Smoldering brown eyes peered out through long strands of chestnut hair. She brushed the hair out of her face and began to clap at the close of the song. The band gave *her* a standing ovation. She grinned somewhat sheepishly and took a bow. After a couple more songs, Kurt yelled down to her to request a song.

Kate yelled up to them, "Still the Night." Sammy said to the crowd, "She wants to hear 'Still the Night.' How about the rest of you?"

The crowd erupted, and the band started the song. It's hard for me to pin down my all-time favorite song, but for a live show, very few beat "Still the Night." However, I must confess that I don't think I've ever heard *the band* sing it live. It's such a popular song that the singing fans usually drown them out. When they finished the song, they said goodnight and left the stage. We didn't move, and neither did anyone else. The chanting began: "BoDeans, BoDeans, BoDeans."

We knew they had to come back. It's the same game that bands play with the fans at every concert in America. The band says goodbye, and the fans chant in the dark. After a few minutes the band comes back out and the encore begins. It happens in every genre of music, at every show. Of course, there was the possibility that the band wouldn't come back. But not tonight. They hadn't played "Good Things." To the delight of the crowd and the surprise of no one, the band emerged from backstage carrying water bottles and waving to the crowd. After a couple of songs, the excited crowd came to a mild hush as the familiar melody drifted up to the evening sky. Kurt reminded the crowd that it was a "sing-along song."

"One, two, three, four," he shouted and the band joined in. "Sunlight fall, down on the field, sunlight fall down over me. Work all day; be all that I can be . . ."

Kate was dancing close again, swaying with the tune. When the chorus came, she joined in with everyone, "No, no, no, don't pass me over. No, no, no, don't pass me by. See, I can see, good things for you and I."

That night it became more than a crowd or radio favorite in Bloomington. That night it would become the theme song of the town. Bloomington was saying to Major League Baseball, "No, no, no, don't pass us over. No, no, no, don't pass us by."

Call it random chance. Call it fate. Call it whatever you want, but a TV reporter from Indianapolis was covering the event. During "Good Things," the cameraman had gone to the side of the stage and was filming the band and the crowd. By some cosmic coincidence, all but two people at the front of the crowd were wearing Trolley Dodgers T-shirts. The reporter and the cameraman took the footage back to the station and ran it with the heading: BLOOMINGTON RESIDENTS SERENADE MAJOR LEAGUE BASEBALL. The next day, it was on CNN and ESPN and the following Monday, the *Today Show* ran the clip.

Within two weeks of the clip running nationally, we nearly doubled the amount of money raised. Major League Baseball and the McGuire family called for a meeting with Trolley Dodgers, Inc., in Chicago to discuss the sale of the team. To say thanks to the BoDeans, we invited them to sing the National Anthem on Opening Day.

TWENTY

There's a Clover on Your Butt

(Money Raised: $210,454,343.35)

"How do you figure this game? You really can't. Just when you think you have, someone throws you a great curveball, and there you are, walking back to the dugout with your head between your legs."

~ *Davy Lopes*

IT WAS NOW TIME TO IMPRESS Major League Baseball and the McGuire family in person. The commissioner had scheduled a meeting in Chicago. Because of a variety of commitments, we didn't go to Indianapolis International Airport together. Darryl and I caught a ride from Roxy. Darryl had scheduled some routine maintenance on his car, and the Yellow Submarine wouldn't start. Roxy had agreed to give us a ride, but insisted we go the long way. Now that she had a taste, she couldn't seem to get racing out of her system.

Klondike and Pete met us at the airport. They had been in Indianapolis the day before soliciting new investors. Because Kate had just flown back from the annual Mary Kay Seminar in Dallas a couple of days before, she had numerous appointments the day of our flight, so she offered to meet us at the airport as well.

Roxy dropped us off in front of the terminal. She said she had too much to do that afternoon to wait for our plane to depart. When she hugged me goodbye, I noticed her gleam just wasn't there. She was smiling, but she looked tired.

"Are you OK?" I asked.

"I'm fine. Go make Bloomington proud," she said. "I love you." She kissed me on the cheek and hugged me a long time.

Once inside, we found Pete and Klondike at the bar. We sat down with them and waited for another twenty minutes for Kate. When she finally arrived, she had a strange look on her face.

"There's a marshmallow in your hair." I couldn't help but point out this oddity. There had to be story behind the Lucky Charms pink heart marshmallow resting just above her right ear. It was glistening—wet from milk.

Kate stood silent for a moment, a little stunned and a lot disheveled. There was a wet spot on her new business suit.

"Are you OK?" I asked.

"I had an accident."

"Was the other driver a short guy, red hair, wearing a green outfit?" Darryl had noticed the marshmallow too.

"I didn't hit anything. A deer ran out in front of me. I went onto the shoulder, hit my brakes, and spun completely around in the gravel."

"Was the deer eating breakfast?" Klondike asked.

"No, I was."

"When?" Pete said.

"When the deer ran out in front of me."

Pete, Darryl, Klondike and I exchanged looks of bewilderment. I'm sure my face had the same puzzled look as the other guys, like dogs trying to figure out where the voices in the radio are coming from. The others were afraid to ask. I'm a reporter. I had to.

"You were eating cereal while you were driving?"

"Yes."

"Not dry cereal out of the box. You were eating cereal in a bowl, in milk, with a spoon?"

"Yes."

"You are the most amazing woman I have ever met."

"Thank you." She smiled.

"And, there's a clover on your butt."

"Maybe I should go to the ladies' room."

"Perhaps that would be best," said Darryl, trying to hold back laughter.

Kate stumbled off towards the women's restroom. As she disappeared through the doorway, we all started laughing. Then laughter turned to questions.

"Klondike, is she your sister?" Pete asked.

"How do you drive and eat *cereal*?" I asked.

Kate was the most composed, confident woman I had ever met. To see her like this was unbelievable. It's not that we delighted in her misery. It's just that seeing someone so refined with marshmallows in her hair is kind of like seeing Haley's Comet. You only get one shot; make the most of it.

Of course, our tradition of nicknaming people had a new victim. Lucky Charms (a.k.a. Kate) emerged from the restroom. Now she was smiling, almost laughing at herself. She was back to looking perfect. As she approached, she could tell we wanted more details and felt composed enough to offer them.

"OK, OK children. I was driving with my knees and eating cereal. I do it all the time and this is the first time I've ever had an accident."

Klondike asked, "What else can you do while you're driving?"

"That's none of your business," she answered as we boarded the plane.

After arriving in Chicago, we made our way to the downtown Omni Hotel where the meeting was to take place. We had made reservations to spend the night in the same hotel, so each of us went to our rooms to freshen up. We met back in the lobby and together were ushered into a meeting room.

If the rest of our group was intimidated, they didn't show it. I was terrified. Standing before us were the commissioner, the players' union representative, and David McGuire. They were flanked on both sides by lawyers as far as the eye could see. Klondike, Darryl, and I were there mostly for moral support. Occasionally we would offer a bit of relevant information. But mostly, this was the Pete and Kate show.

For forty-five minutes they dazzled the MLB brass with financial forecasts, stadium blueprints, and the plans for moving the team. The commissioner seemed most concerned with the stadium design and the timetable for moving the team. The players' representative was more concerned with the town. He said repeatedly that we were going to have a difficult time attracting free agents to Bloomington. McGuire had only one thing on his mind: money. "We've set a deadline of September 1. You will have to raise at least the minimum amount by then. I say 'at least' because Roland Green will most likely bid higher than the asking price."

An alarm bell went off in my head when he made that statement. What if this had never been about a competition between the Mega Media Corporation and Bloomington? What if Major League Baseball never intended to seriously consider our proposal, but really was helping the McGuires drive up Green's bid? Ominous music began playing in my head.

"We feel confident that we can raise that much and more. All we can say is wait until September and see how our bid compares to Green's," said Pete.

After a few more questions and answers, the meeting concluded. The commissioner agreed to release a statement to the effect that MLB continued to view us as a serious contender to buy the Dodgers and that they would be making an official visit to Bloomington soon. Everyone stood up, shook hands, and began to file out of the room. I wanted to corner McGuire and ask him straight up, "Are we just helping you run up the price on Green?" But my chance never came.

I didn't voice my feelings to anyone else in the group. They were excited about the results and I didn't want to bring them down. After a few hours, I dismissed the idea as paranoia and joined in the celebration. We stayed Saturday and Sunday in Chicago to watch the Cubs play St. Louis.

By late Sunday afternoon, we were eager to get home and share our success with the town. The commissioner's press release would bring in new investors. Big changes were on the horizon, but not all of them were good.

TWENTY-ONE

The Art in Me

(Money Raised: $239,372,113.35)

"A life is not important except in the impact it has on other lives."

~ *Jackie Robinson*

I REMEMBER A DAY WHEN I was really little, maybe four or five, a time when I was still too little to play baseball with the older kids. My parents had dropped me off at Roxy's, and a game was going on in her yard. When the older kids wouldn't let me play, Roxy took my hand in hers and convinced me to go for a walk. We left the house and the game, passed all the homes on her block, and found a trail that led into a small forest.

As we walked, Roxy told me stories of Jackie Robinson, Mickey Mantle, and Ernie Banks. About fifty yards into the forest, she left the path and pushed through some trees and brush to an opening. Out of shadow we emerged into a large clearing. The center was lit up by the July sun and the border was lined with raspberry bushes except for the opening we had pushed through.

She produced a canvas bag from under the arm that wasn't holding my hand. We then proceeded to pick raspberries until the bag was full. Before we returned, we sat in the middle for a while, soaking up the sun.

"Do you know why I didn't make those boys pick you for the game?" she asked. It didn't occur to me until just then that it was her yard; she could have forced the older kids to let me play.

"No. How come?"

"I let the game go on because I wanted you to learn something important. Those boys are much bigger, and you're not ready to play with them yet. If you had played with them, you may have been discouraged and never wanted to play baseball again. I don't want you to be afraid to play against bigger boys, but you need to learn how first. You need to learn how to hit, and throw, and run. And you need to know the rules. Do you understand?"

"I guess so," I answered. I doubt that I really did at the time, but as I grew older, I could understand her wisdom. Then I asked, "Grandma, who was the best ever?"

"Well some say Babe Ruth, some say Willie Mays, and some folks think it was Ted Williams. But I never saw those guys play. The best I ever saw were Jackie Robinson and Ernie Banks. You could see the art in them."

"You could see what on them?"

"Art, and not on them, in them."

"What do you mean?"

"God puts art in everybody. Some folks you can see it pretty easily. Others you have to look real hard. But it's there, *if you look.*" I was really confused. "There was art in the way Jackie stole bases. There was art in the way Ernie played defense and hit home runs. The art comes from doing things with passion. It comes from hard work and developing your God-given talents. And it comes from being true to yourself."

"Do I have art on me?"

"No, you have raspberry juice *on* you. But, yes, there is art *in* you. The way you picked those raspberries had art in it."

"Do you have art *on* you?" I asked. My five-year-old mind couldn't get the in/on concept down.

"Well, let's go home and turn these raspberries into a pie. Then you'll see the art in me."

That was the first lesson Roxy taught me that I can remember. There were many more after that. What I didn't realize then, and was oblivious to for most of my adult life, was that many people were touched by the art in Roxy.

When I arrived home Sunday night, the smile that had been plastered on my face from our successful trip to Chicago disappeared when I played my phone messages. A couple messages from my parents said to call them right away. They didn't say why. I knew after playing a couple more messages. The next message I remember said, "Sorry about Roxy." Things got blurry and distorted after that. I know I called my parents and we talked for an hour. I have no idea what we said to each other.

When we were done, I remember collapsing on my couch. It was hard to breathe, as if the wind had been knocked out of me. I couldn't imagine a world without Roxy, but that's exactly where I was living now. I suspect I cried a little.

She died in her car—probably the way she would have wanted to go. Apparently when she returned to Bloomington from the airport, she ran a few errands for The Salvation Army. She arrived home just as the sun slipped behind the trees. Roxy pulled into the driveway and turned off the car. As the engine came to a stop, so did her heart. I was told she didn't feel a thing. None of us knew until we got back to Bloomington Sunday night.

Nothing I've ever lost hurt more than losing Roxy. She taught me how to live. She reminded me to breathe, laugh, and sing. Most of all she taught me to follow my dreams. So whatever doubts or misgivings I had about trying to buy the Dodgers were washed away when she died. I did it for Bloomington. I did it for me. But mostly, I did it for Roxy.

Monday morning I awoke to the phone ringing. I was face down on the couch wearing the same clothes from Sunday.

"Hello."

"It's Darryl. I just heard about Roxy. Man, I'm sorry."

"Thanks."

"Are you OK?"

"I'm numb. It doesn't seem real. She was so active, so healthy."

"What are you going to do now? Are you going to work?"

"No, I better call and tell them."

"All right, I already called in to say I wouldn't be at work. I'll come over and pick you up in an hour."

When Roxy died, Darryl had lost a grandmother too. Roxy had treated him like one of her own throughout our lives. His real grandparents had died before he was born, so Roxy really was his grandmother. I knew he was hurting just as bad as I was.

While I was taking a shower, Kate and a couple of other people left messages. I didn't return any of the calls. I just didn't feel much like talking. Darryl didn't either. When he picked me up, we drove in silence to Adams Funeral Home. My parents were already waiting and we worked on the funeral arrangements. After lunch, I had Darryl drop me off at work. I decided I had to write something about Roxy's life for the next day's paper. An obituary had already been written, but it had not yet been run. So I added the following paragraphs to the end:

She arrived on July 27, 1925. The doctor who performed the delivery claimed that when spanked, Roxy Marie Robinson laughed instead of crying. From birth, she laughed more than she cried. It's not that she had a life of ease. Some might think she had a tragic life, one that would have left most people bitter. But Roxy lived life to its fullest, no matter what hand she was dealt.

She understood that life wasn't about money or possessions, things she never had in abundance. Friendships were her most treasured keepsakes, and of Roxy's friends the count was beyond measure. She saw the art in others, and taught us to do the same.

The huge crowd at the funeral proved the last sentences of the obituary true. Even Mayor Gomez was in attendance. My parents got to meet Kate. They were impressed. I slipped back into that place where nothing seems real. It was as if I were watching the whole thing on TV. It just couldn't be real. But it was. Later that afternoon, my dad showed me Roxy's will. After a lot of legal garbage, there were two simple lines at the end. "To my grandson Andy, I leave my baseball diamond. He can also have the house attached to it. "

Roxy's yard was sacred ground. For the children who passed the summers playing baseball in her side yard, it might as well have been the Garden of Eden, and her house a cathedral. Now that cathedral had a broken stained-glass window.

After the funeral, I excused myself from the rest of my family and drove to Roxy's house. I parked my car and started to walk up the street. Fighting back tears, I made my way past all the homes on her block and over to what used to be the forest. Several housing developments had shrunk it to a fraction of its original size. I remember thinking that maybe the DWARVES were on to something with this whole save-the-environment thing. But, the path was still there. And the tree that marked where to leave the path was there as well. Pushing through the brush, I stepped into the opening that had provided many getaways over the years, not to mention many raspberry pies.

I stayed there until sundown, talking to myself, God, and Roxy. I imagined that she was in heaven, entertaining the angels just like she entertained everyone she met down here. I realized that day what inspired the art in me. It was Roxy.

TWENTY-TWO

Two Hundred Fifty Million (In Mostly Small Bills)

(Money Raised: $250,000,003.35)

> "It was Brooklyn against the world. They were not only complete fanatics, but they knew baseball like the fans of no other city. It was exciting to play there. It was a treat. I walked into that crummy, flyblown park as Brooklyn manager for nine years, and every time I entered, my pulse quickened and my spirits soared."
>
> ~ *Leo Durocher*

WHY IS MY PHONE RINGING? It was early on a Saturday morning. No one I knew would have the guts to call me this early on a Saturday. Ignore it; go back to sleep. The ringing stopped and I returned to a dream. I was pitching for the Dodgers. But I was wearing a sombrero on the mound. It sort of flopped up and down when I went into my windup. I delivered a splitter and Barry Bonds started to swing. Just as the ball was about to make contact . . . RING!

"What!" I yelled to whoever was on the line. I reached for the phone and grabbed a picture, then a glass, then a baseball, finally the phone.

"Hello."

"We did it!" It was a female voice.

"Yes, we did. And whatever it was we did, I'm sure we can do it again after I've had more sleep. Goodbye."

"No, wait! We did it! We raised the money! Enough to buy the Dodgers!"

"Who is this?"

"KATE!"

"We did it?"

"Yes! Get out of bed and get over here!"

"OK. Wait, where's 'here'?"

"I'm at Trolley Dodgers headquarters. We're calling all the board members now. We're holding a news conference in a couple hours!"

"All right. I'm on my way."

It had been two weeks since Roxy died. Consumed with grief, I had buried myself in work at the newspaper and had lost track of how much money had been raised. This was the first good news I had heard since the Chicago trip. I quickly got ready and went downtown.

The scene at headquarters was electric. People were hugging and going crazy. Kate had notified all of the local radio stations, two of which already had vans on the Square doing live remotes. The police blocked off the roads around the Square at the request of Mayor Gomez. Impromptu celebrations broke out all over the city.

It was a party. All morning long, people crowded onto the courthouse lawn and along the streets and sidewalks surrounding The Square.

At eleven, Kate began the news conference. It was carried on ESPN, CNN, all the major networks and most of the Los Angeles radio stations. "I have a prepared statement and then I will take questions. As of this morning, Trolley Dodgers, Inc., has sold enough shares to place a bid on the Los Angeles Dodgers. As we are bidding against Mega Media Network and Mr. Roland Green, I will not disclose the exact dollar amount we have raised. However, it does exceed the minimum threshold required by MLB. A formal bid has been sent to the league office first, per their request, and it will be forwarded to the McGuire family. The bid price was set by our board of directors at a contingency meeting last week. Details of the bid will not be made public until such time as the bid is accepted or rejected by the current owners. Now I will accept questions."

"What will happen to the money if you are turned down?"

"Each individual investor will receive his money back."

"What about the expenses you've incurred? Won't you have to deduct money from the investors?"

"No, the board of directors voted to deduct expenses from the principal amount each board member invested. We wanted to make it clear all along to investors that *we, not they*, were taking the biggest risk in courting the Dodgers to move to Bloomington. Next question?"

"When do you expect to hear from MLB?"

"We expect written acknowledgement that they are in receipt of the bid by Tuesday, and an announcement later in the week."

"If Green's bid is higher, will you be allowed to raise your bid?"

"Yes, but we feel our offer is a winning bid."

"If it isn't, how much higher are you willing to go?"

"I can't answer that question. It would reveal too much of our strategy and this battle isn't over yet."

After a few more questions, Kate turned the podium over to Pete. The rest of the board members had things under control, so she and I left headquarters and walked hand-in-hand around the downtown square. Everywhere we looked, people were celebrating. For one day at least, the people of Bloomington forgot their differences and celebrated *together*.

We spent the day downtown. Most of our time was at headquarters, fielding phone calls and answering questions. Although the downtown party went well into the night, we closed the office at five-thirty. "So, have I *earned* the right to take you to Janko's yet?" I asked.

"I think that would be the perfect way to celebrate today," she answered. We made the short walk west to Janko's and waited for a table. After about twenty minutes, we were seated.

"It's so wonderful to finally have an intimate moment with you," I said.

"This isn't intimate."

"It isn't?"

"We're in the middle of Janko's."

"Yes, but it's a table for two."

"In the middle of a dozen other tables for two . . . and four . . . and six . . ."

"Ah, but they're planning on paying for their dinner," I said.

"And we're not?"

"I thought we'd make a run for it."

"And why is that?" she asked.

"I certainly didn't think *you* should have to pay for it."

"I'm not paying for it and we're not pulling a dine-and-dash in this restaurant."

"OK, but a candlelit dinner followed by danger and intrigue could be very romantic."

"It could land us in jail."

"Well, I'm not in the mood for prison romance, so I guess I'll pay the check," I said. After dinner, we rejoined the celebration on the Square. Bloomington Trolley Dodgers pennants, T-shirts, and other items were everywhere. Somehow we found Darryl in the crowd. Kate spotted some friends and left us standing on the grass by the courthouse.

"Do you believe in shooting stars now?" he asked.

"We don't have a signed contract yet," I answered. "Maybe this celebration is a little premature."

"Does it matter?"

"What do you mean?"

Darryl explained. "Even if we get outbid, even if the Dodgers never move to Bloomington, it doesn't matter. What matters is that the whole world laughed at us when we said we were going to raise enough money to buy the Dodgers. But we didn't give up. We didn't let our differences derail our dream. That's bigger than a baseball team."

"So for you, it was never about the Dodgers?" I asked.

"No, for me and you, it was always about the Dodgers," he said. "For Bloomington it became something bigger." He left me to think about what he said. I sat down on a bench and watched the celebration. Someone had arranged a last-minute fireworks show. I stared at the sky, watching little pinpoints of fire travel up to explode in gold and blue and red.

Maybe Darryl was right. Maybe a dream, pursued with passion and single-mindedness, elevates a person or a group beyond the mundane. It takes them to a dimension where they are really alive—to a place where they can achieve things that really matter. However, where would that leave this town if we were to fail? We were unified that night. Would we stay unified if the trolley passed us by?

TWENTY-THREE

Lawn Seats

> "The field was even greener than my boy's mind had pictured it. In later years, friends of ours visited Ireland and said the grass there was plenty green alright, but that not even the Emerald Isle itself was as green as the grass that grew in Ebbets Field."
>
> ~ *Duke Snider*

A week before the deadline, I turned on ESPN in the break room at the *Daily News* to hear MLB announce that a press conference would be held that afternoon to discuss the sale of the Los Angeles Dodgers. I made a quick call to Kate, who knew nothing about it. A few more phone calls confirmed that none of the board members were aware of it either. I began to worry. Maybe it was just an update by the commissioner. I tried all morning to suppress what I was really thinking—had the McGuires taken the offer from Green?

I was too nervous to eat. My stomach was in knots. An hour before the press conference, I told my boss that I was going to cover the press conference at Trolley Dodgers headquarters. When I arrived at the north side of the Square, every spot was filled. I wound up parking two blocks north of the Square and walking back to Trolley Dodgers, Inc. When I arrived, Kate and nearly all the board members were inside. Many of the small investors were there, too. Darryl was on the radio, and everyone was taking turns listening to him and watching ESPN. Kate was sitting on her desk next to Klondike. I sat on the desk next to her and she grabbed my arm, not letting go. She looked me in the eyes and said nothing. She was scared. It was the first time I'd seen any hint of fear in her. It made me uncomfortable.

At three o'clock, we turned the audio down on Darryl's show. ESPN's anchor explained that they were getting ready to go live to Chavez Ravine, where the Dodgers were holding a news conference. The first image said it all. I didn't need to hear a word. In fact, I didn't. I went into what I can only describe as a trance. Nothing seemed real. It was like I was having an out-of-body experience. There on the screen was the acting commissioner of baseball. To his right was David McGuire. To his left was Roland Green. Mega Media Network had bought the Dodgers.

Kate put her head on my shoulder and sobbed. Grown men all over the office wiped away tears, shocked at the screen and sickened in their disbelief. But I couldn't hear any of it. It had to be a bad dream.

I grabbed Kate's hand and whispered, "I'm leaving."

"Please don't go," Kate pleaded.

"It's just too much. First Roxy and now this. I need to be alone for a while."

I let go of her hand and walked out the door. It was cloudy now, as if the news had stolen the sun along with our dreams. I walked slowly to my car. I couldn't hear the sounds of the traffic around me. I could see the lightning, the pedestrians opening umbrellas. I could see the huge drops of rain, polka-dotting the sidewalk below me. But I couldn't hear the thunder, or the thunderstorm overtaking the city. I reached my car before I was completely wet.

I drove south for I don't know how long. I made aimless turns through neighborhoods, by businesses, down alleys. I finally stopped the car, realizing I was at Bryan Park. With no idea where I was going or why, I crossed the park to the softball diamonds and sat under some trees next to the trail. The thunderstorm was still raging and I wasn't in a safe place. I don't know how long I sat there, but when I came to my senses, a dog was licking me on the face. I realized two college girls who had been walking their dog had stopped to see if I was OK. The rain had stopped. I couldn't say how long ago, but I was still very wet. I got up and made my way to my car. When I started the car, the dashboard clock said nine-thirty. I had checked out of reality for six hours. It was the same feeling I'd had only a few weeks ago when Roxy died. On my way home, I noticed that the storm had knocked down some trees and power lines, making the trip a bit more eventful than usual.

When I finally got home, my phone was ringing. I ignored it along with the numerous messages on my answering machine. I just dried off, changed clothes and went to bed. The next morning, Kate called.

"Hello."

"It's me. Are you OK?"

"No, how about you?"

"I've been better. Are you going to work today?"

"I will eventually. How about you?"

"Yeah, I'm going to the Trolley Dodgers office. We have to start sending people's money back." Her voice started to crack with the last couple of words.

"Have we heard anything from the league, the McGuires? Why didn't we get a chance to counter offer?"

"I don't know. I just don't know."

When I arrived at the newspaper, there were messages all over my desk. I made some calls to MLB, the Dodgers, and a few moles I had in other organizations. Everyone basically said the same thing: we never had a chance. We simply served as a tool for driving up the asking price.

I wrote three stories about the sale. After each one was finished, I hit delete and started over. Each one was a version of the same thing: trashing the league and complaining about the unfairness of the process. Why didn't they wait until the first of September? Why didn't they allow us to counter offer?

Then I wrote the version that made the paper. I described the terms of the sale with no sour grapes and congratulated the new owner. I thanked ESPN for keeping us in the national spotlight with the daily ticker. Then I thanked all the people who invested whether they gave large sums or just bought a few shares. Finally, I reminded the town of what we had accomplished in the last three months. The last paragraph summed up the whole summer:

Three months ago, a handful of Bloomington residents had a dream. That dream had three major components: to unify the town, to raise a lot of money, and to buy the Dodgers. We failed to buy the Dodgers, and we're giving back the money. So that leaves us with each other. Our differences didn't seem so bad when we had a common goal. Going forward, maybe they still won't seem so bad.

I filed my story and went home. I took Friday off and didn't answer the phone. On Saturday afternoon, someone knocked on my door. I opened it to find Kate standing in a white tank top and cut-off denim shorts. Her hair was pulled back in a ponytail, which slid through the opening of an Indians baseball cap.

"Come on," she said, "we're taking a drive."

"Where to?"

"Indy."

"What for?"

"Because, you have to get out of this apartment."

"OK."

I wasn't in the mood to go to Indianapolis, but I didn't have the energy to argue. I was still pretty deflated.

"Are we going to a game?"

"Yes."

I thought so. I went back to my room to change clothes. This time I didn't care that I left her in a messy living room. I grabbed a black Indians golf shirt out of the closet, the last clean shirt I owned. I switched from jeans to khaki shorts and changed shirts. My favorite Indians hat had been lost saving Kate from the bagels and bubblegum. I located my backup Indians hat and headed out to face the world. The only clue to the outside world that I hadn't left my apartment for two days was my unshaven face.

Kate insisted on driving. She seemed to have a plan.

"What time is the game?"

"Seven."

"We're leaving a little early, aren't we?" I asked. "Did you want to see batting practice?"

"No, I thought we would take the long way."

As she pulled away from my apartment, I fumbled through her CD case for a minute or two until I found *Home* by the BoDeans. As the slow guitar lead-in opened track number six I rolled down the window. "There's two boys holding, stars for wishing . . ." That was Darryl and me. "One boy's sure, one says I don't know." It was like they wrote the song while watching us when we were twelve. How many times had I listened to that song and never made the connection? The chorus was simple, "You don't get much without giving." It repeated again and again in my head until the light bulb finally went off.

We had just passed Assembly Hall and Memorial Stadium, and caught a glimpse of the IU football team practicing. "Don't turn on Dunn Street. Take me over to Roxy's house first," I sort of shouted. "I'm sorry. It will make sense when we get there."

Kate gave me the strangest look, but crossed through Dunn Street and drove across town to Roxy's. When I got there, there were a few kids sitting in the yard. A couple threw a ball back and forth. A few more children were circling aimlessly on their bikes. All of them sprang to life when they saw us pull in to Roxy's gravel driveway. "Hey Andy," said one of the boys. "Sorry about the Dodgers."

"Yeah, no more Gomez Park," said another boy. "No more trolleys. That stinks!"

His sister said, "We sure miss Roxy."

"I do too," I said. "But the city council is keeping the trolleys. And there is going to be a Gomez Park. And the Trolley Dodgers will be playing there."

Nine children stared at me in disbelief. I tossed Kate the key to the storage shed. "Could you open that, so these ballplayers can get to their equipment?"

"I sure can," she answered.

While Kate was getting the equipment, I unlocked the side door to Roxy's garage and searched inside for a few minutes. It didn't take long for me to find a sign she had used for a yard sale and a can of spray paint. I returned to the kids and Kate, all of whom were bursting with anticipation. I planted the sign in the yard and spray-painted "Gomez Park" over the faded letters from the yard sale. The kids let out a huge cheer.

"Kate, do we have any Trolley Dodgers T-shirts left in your trunk?" I asked.

"Sure, there's a whole box of them."

I opened her trunk and pulled out the box. Each of the kids got a T-shirt; on the youngest ones they looked like dresses. "You guys are the Trolley Dodgers now, and this is your stadium. I'll put up a better sign when I have more time." I gave the oldest boy the key to the shed and told him where to hide it. The wiffle ball games had ended when Roxy died. Now her side yard was a ballpark again. Over the next few months, I would make numerous improvements to Gomez Park, but I never installed lights. With lights, the games could have gone longer, but they might have kept kids of all ages from seeing shooting stars.

We left the kids to their game and made our way back across town to take the long way to Indianapolis. Over the next hour and a half, neither of us spoke very much. We made our way north on Dunn Street to where it meets Lake Griffey. Just below the dam on the lake's western edge, we passed the dog park, filled with pure breeds, mongrels and other canines of questionable origin, many resembling their masters. We reached Old State Road 37 and turned right, heading up the steep hill that Roxy must have driven a thousand times. At the top of the hill, the road starts to gently break away from the lake and steadily makes its way north.

If nature is a gift, then this Indiana highway is the ribbon on the box. Follow its twists and turns and you can see some beautiful countryside. Steep hills give way to lush valleys. Farmlands border vast forests, and lakes are hidden along the way. In fall, the turning of the leaves makes a spectacular backdrop for the Hilly Hundred, an annual bike tour that attracts hundreds of participants.

But this was late summer, and everything was green and ripe and vivid. We passed cornfields that were getting ready for harvest; fields of soybeans, too. The farmland gave way to hills again, and we climbed up through a shadow of trees. To the right was a great ravine, and to the left were trailer homes, some barely visible through the trees. I began to wonder how many Olympic gymnasts or professional acrobats were from Indiana because there seemed to be a lot of trampolines.

At the bottom of the hill, we emerged through the trees and into a large valley. On the left, the road followed the hill down and back up on the far side. To the right, the valley was home to a cattle farm. A herd of cows occupied a green pasture. Some stood and others lounged near a stream that wound through the pasture and off to the far end of the valley. A couple of horses were in the pasture as well. They looked bored. I would have offered them a ride to the game, but it didn't seem like their kind of fun.

Eventually we made our way to the Hoosier National Forest with stretches through parts of Morgan and Monroe Counties. We wound through the forest until it opened onto more farmland. We were only a few minutes from where the old highway meets the new. Roxy always hated knowing the old road was about to end. So did I.

I noticed on the left a brightly painted building that stood out from the rest of the homes on that stretch of road. A lighted sign explained the rainbow-colored anomaly—"Clown School," it read.

Kate beat me to the punch. "You know, if you went in there and told them all of your accomplishments, I bet they would give you an honorable doctorate."

"Well if you learn how to make balloon animals, I can get you on the Future Carnies' float next year."

"No thanks," she answered. "I'm definitely going on the bagel float. They had better projectiles."

"But the troubadours had the beer."

"Yeah, and no way to defend themselves," she pointed out. "I'll stick with the bagels."

"Well, you got me there."

When we arrived at Victory Field, we parked at the White River State Park lot and crossed over to the stadium. We were still early enough that we didn't have to wait long in line. We purchased lawn seats and made our way through the turnstiles and out on to the concourse. The Columbus Clippers were taking batting practice as we made our way past left field towards center.

Kate caught my hand. "Where do you want to sit?"

"I prefer the right field grass."

We continued around, passing the tee-pee just to the left of the center field ticket gates. As we got closer to the right field grass, familiar faces appeared. On a sea of blankets sat Klondike, Bonnie, and the girls. Next to them were Darryl, Melissa, and their kids. We spread our blanket next to Klondike's at the insistence of his daughters. I sat down and Abby jumped into my lap.

Toby Newman was taking batting practice for the Clippers. "Hey, is that Newby that used to play for the Rangers?" I asked. "Wow! He's turned into a tub of goo."

On his last cut, he drove the ball into right field and half-heartedly jogged to first base. "Yeah," said Darryl. "Look at that twinkie run."

"You Freddys," Klondike said. "He's coming off knee surgery. He couldn't help it if he packed on a few extra pounds."

"No, he's pretty much a tub of goo," said a voice from behind us. I turned around to see Pete holding a couple of beers and Maple, I mean Martha, holding a blanket which she spread on the ground next to ours.

And so the player analysis went, right up until the national anthem. The grieving period was over. We had pursued the dream, and it didn't work out. But we had tried and it had been worth the ride. We were the four Freddys again. We had returned to less lofty pursuits. But along the way we had gained two new Freddys, "Fredettes" if you will. One was a National Sales Director for Mary Kay who had taken to hanging out with the likes of us. And the other was a vegan, who had once hit me over the head with a cafeteria tray. Only in Bloomington.

A few innings into the game, I caught Kate staring at me.

"What?"

"I can't believe you're actually doing that and not getting grossed out," she said. Abby had been sucking the salt out of the shelled peanuts and then handing them back to me. I would crack them open and eat the nuts.

"Abby and I are a team," I answered. "Right Abs?" I held my hand up, and Abby gave me a high five. She then poked me in the chest with the bill of her Indians hat.

"You're going to make a good father some day."

I reached for my drink, which Abby almost knocked over, but didn't answer Kate.

"You'll also make a good husband," she said, sort of stumbling over the words. She had a really strange look on her face. I took a big gulp from my drink.

"What I'm trying to say is, you'll make a good husband for *me* someday."

I spit Coke all over the blanket.

ABOUT THE AUTHOR

JEFF STANGER LIVES and writes in Indianapolis for reasons that aren't entirely clear. Prior to that he lived in Bloomington, IN where he managed to find time to graduate from Indiana University and write a popular sports column for *BC Magazine*.

His classic works of fiction were all written in chalk on the sidewalks of Bloomington and Indianapolis. Being the first (and only) chalk novelist has earned him a place in Indiana lore as either a passionate artist or just a really odd person, depending on your point of view. After years of cranking out such sidewalk hits as *View from the Pavement* and *Short Stories in a Cul-De-Sac* he gave in to pressure from his adoring fans (both of them) and embarked on his first "traditional" novel.

In his professional life, he is a well-sought grant consultant for nonprofits in the Midwest. He also serves on the Board of Directors for Play Ball Indiana, an organization dedicated to providing inner-city youth with opportunities to play baseball. His blog, "Jeffreaux's World" is a popular internet destination.

Want more?
Visit
www.trolleydodgers.com